DEAR READER,

I am pleased to finally be able to bring you this chipper, cheeky little novella, which is one of the first things I ever wrote, many years ago, as a fledgling romance writer. It was born as an homage to one of my favorite 'caper movies,' "How to Steal a Million," written by Harry Kurnitz, based on a story by George Bradshaw, directed by William Wyler, and starring the incomparable Audrey Hepburn and a dashing Peter O'Toole. I hope my version of the story retains all the madcap charm of the original, while giving you a different, but no less satisfying and amusing experience. Enjoy!

Wishing you all happy reading!

Cheers,

Elizabeth

My gift to you!

Rebecca,

Mad For Love

Haris to happily ever after!

HIGHLAND BRIDES, BOOK 1

ELIZABETH ESSEX

Elizabeth Essex

MAD FOR LOVE
Copyright © 2015 by Elizabeth Essex
Excerpt from *Mad About the Marquess* by Elizabeth Essex, 2015
Excerpt from *Mad, Bad, and Dangerous to Marry* by Elizabeth Essex, 2015
Cover design by Patricia Schmitt/PickyMe Artist
Cover photo by Jenn LeBlanc/Studio Smexy
Vector images used under Creative Commons Attribution License: BSGStudio on All-Free-Download; Webdesignhot on All-Free-Download

ERB Publishing

ISBN: 978-0-9969881-7-9
For information, address Elizabeth Essex at elizabethessex.com

DEDICATION

To Chris Keniston and Kathy Ivan,
authors and friends, for shepherding me through.

Chapter 1

London, Early Spring 1790

MARIE CHANTAL AMÉLIE du Blois never felt more French than when she was in London. Something about her seemed to mark her as different, as if the nightmare of their flight from Paris were painted across her face instead of the polite English smile she tried to give the world. As if her full French mouth were incapable of a sufficiently stiff upper lip.

But despite this deformity of character, she would continue to try to stiffen her lip, continue to wear English clothes and buy English bread while she shopped in English markets—she would become English through sheer dint of will.

Because she loved London.

She loved everything about the damp, down-at-her-heels city. Papa often said that London was dull in comparison to Paris, with all its fashion and art, but Mignon, as Papa called her, liked dull. She liked safe. And London's shabby pavements, leafy squares, and tidy shops felt entirely safe.

"Good morning, Miss Blois." Mrs. Parkhurst, from the house next door, nodded cordially as Mignon came along the uneven pavement.

Soho Square wasn't the most fashionable district of London, or the richest. But it would do very nicely. Because it was pretty, and green, and nothing bad could ever happen here, so far away, across the water from Paris, where bad things seemed to be happening daily.

"*Madame.*" Mignon curtsied and shifted her market basket to the other hip. "How do you fare this fine morning?"

"Tolerably well," Mrs. Parkhurst nodded her billowing English bonnet. "You are to be congratulated. I saw your father, earlier. He seemed very well pleased by the auction of his art at Mr. Christie's."

"Auction?" Mignon felt her stiffened upper lip fall slack. This was the first she had heard of an auction.

"Very pleased, he was." Mrs. Parkhurst was nodding in her genial way. "So nice to see him so pleased and well, after all your troubles."

Their 'troubles' had been broadcast about the square like poppy seeds by Papa. In his version of the truth, they had left France under the most horrific of circumstances. True, there was great turmoil and unrest in that country, especially for aristocrats, even disgraced youngest sons of disinherited younger sons—in Paris the slightest whiff of aristocratic forbearers had been enough to incite a mob. But the plain truth was, she and Papa had managed to escape before the worst of the violence had found them. Because her papa, bless him, was a scoundrel, and scoundrels had a nose for such things.

"Thank you kindly, *Madame.*" Mignon made the lady a graceful curtsy. "I am glad the weather continues fine for your walk. Good day."

The old woman nodded regally, pleased that she had been the one to bring Mignon the news, and made her way onward while Mignon bounded up the shallow step of Number 30, through the unlocked door—Papa may have said London was boring, but he gloried in the fact that in Soho Square, he could leave his door unlocked—and into the neat, neoclassical foyer. "Good afternoon, Henri. Is my father at home?"

Their major domo took her wide-brimmed straw hat and York tan gloves. "In his chambers, *Mademoiselle*," he said in his heavily accented English. "Do you care for tea?"

"No, thank you, Henri. I will go straight up." Mignon picked up the skirts of her walking dress, and mounted the stair to the top floor where her father kept his rooms, including a secret studio reached only by a hidden passage through Papa's enormous *armoire*.

"Papa?" She stepped into his glass-roofed *atelier*, hidden from view of the street, at the back of the roof.

"Mignon!" he called with his usual Gallic enthusiasm. "Hello, my darling."

"Papa." She tried to make her greeting stern. Still, he was her papa, and force of habit made her kiss him on both cheeks in the French manner. "Papa, it becomes necessary for us to have a long, serious talk."

"Aha!" His smile was sly and gleeful. "You heard of my triumph."

"It is all over the street, Papa. You should not talk of money to such people as Mrs. Parkhurst—it's not done. She will put it about that we are vulgar."

"Pah! We are French," he countered, dismissing all notions of English propriety. "We can never be vulgar. Oh, my angel, I wish I had thought to take you. It was a triumph, the sale. I could have sold a score of Vermeers on the very spot, had I put them up for auction."

"Papa," she made her voice chiding. "One Vermeer is more than enough. Papa, you must stop."

He winced, closing his eyes the way he always did when he didn't want to listen. "Move out of my light." He waved her over to a chair. "I must finish this work while the heat of success lends me genius."

A peek at his canvas revealed him putting the finishing details on another oil, a portrait of a lace be-decked cavalier, painted in the Dutch style—another forgery, no matter the style.

"Papa, it is too soon!"

"Never fear, my child. This long lost masterpiece from the Blois collection will not be for sale for many, many years. I will hang it in the salon, and then perhaps, in good time, some rich-as-Croesus English lord may persuade me to part with it."

"Papa." Mignon heaved out a resigned sigh. "You are such a scoundrel."

Her papa was entirely unrepentant. "Thank you, my child."

He went back to his work, while she tried to think of a new argument to sway him from his crooked path. Which was highly unlikely, because none of her arguments had ever made the slightest impression upon her Papa.

"There." He put down the brushes. "It is done." He turned the easel to present her the canvas.

Mignon turned her own critical eye to the piece. "Hals?"

"Aha! Yes, very good, my dear. Yes, I doubt even Frans Hals himself would be able to tell the different between his *Cavalier* and mine."

"One can only assume the reason he does not do so is because he is dead," Mignon muttered before she tried a different approach. "You know, Papa, this boastfulness is entirely unbecoming." She busied herself tidying up the perpetual mess of the *atelier*—Papa never let Henri in to clean. "Someday, you are not going to be able to contain your terrible pride." She picked up a particularly dirty plate.

"Ahh, *non*!" He snatched the plate back. "My dirt. Careful." He stored the tea saucer carefully in a cabinet. "That is not ordinary dirt. It is Hals dirt. Dutch dirt. I have cultivated it from the backs of these ancient canvases." He picked up one of the small oil paintings 'liberated' from Papa's cousin, the *comte*'s *hotel* in Paris—one amongst the few such small paintings they had been able to conceal and bring to London just as the revolution began.

Because scoundrels like her papa were always able to smell the stink of trouble on the wind far better than honest men like her dear dead cousin.

"I have to scrape it off, you see"—he demonstrated his

technique by taking a stiff brush to the back of the canvas—
"and mix it with my pigments and oils from Holland for the
Dutch masters. I use the Masaccio"—he gestured to a tiny,
jewel-like *Madonna and Child*—"for my Italian paintings, so
all their scholars and experts cannot possibly tell the
difference. Haha!" He could not contain his glee at the
thought. "Science is nothing compared to art!"

And art was nothing compared to commerce. And
commerce did not like to be duped—it would get resentful.
"Papa, you cannot go on producing an infinite supply of
Hals and Vermeers."

He waved away her concern. "True, there are others just
as deserving of my genius. But think, my darling—in his
lifetime, Vermeer was always poor and in debt, while I, in
loving homage to his great genius, have bought myself this
house, and live in style! You like living in such style, don't
you?"

She liked living quietly, which was almost impossible
with her papa. "Papa, that is not the point. I keep telling
you, when you sell a forged masterpiece, it is a crime."

"But I don't sell them to poor people. I sell them to rich
aristocrats, and they get something for their trouble—they
get great art! I give them taste! I help them become the great
men they want to be seen as by giving them this art, this
caché."

"It is a public service then, is it?"

Papa was immune to sarcasm. "They should give me a
knighthood."

"They are more like to give you a swim in the Channel.
And then where will you be? Having a very one-sided
conversation with *Madame Guillotine*."

"Pah." He shrugged such negative thoughts off. "Then
we will go to America. I'm told the Americans are in great
need of art, and in even greater need of taste."

Chapter 2

RORY CATHCART KNEW he was about to do something he would live to regret the moment he opened his front door. But that didn't bother him in the least. Because his three best friends in all the world were standing on the other side. And such a ramshackle assemblage always meant for trouble.

The best kind of trouble.

Damn, but he was glad to see them. London had been a lonely place without friends this past winter. But it would never do to tell them so.

"Ain't ye fellows got any manners," he drawled from the doorstep. "This isn't Edinburgh. In London, one doesn't impose oneself before breakfast."

"Don't be absurd." Alasdair Colquhoun, heir to the Marquess of Cairn, and lifelong damned wonderful pain in the arse, brushed by without waiting to be invited in. "It's nearly noon, ye lazy hoist."

"Do come in." Rory waved the other two—his two other school chums, Ewan and Archie—in. "Not that it would do any good to try and keep ye three manky skivers out."

"Never has." Ewan Cameron, Duke of Crieff, shook Rory's hand, and signaled to the carriage in the street. "By the way, we're moving in."

"What, all of ye skiving blighters?" Rory used the blunt Scots rudeness to keep his delight from his tone. "A call is one thing, but an encampment is entirely another. Hain't ye got enough blunt to get yer own digs?"

"Certainly, but where would be the fun in that?" Ewan slapped him consolingly on the back. "And Alasdair already has his own place, though it's not quite so nice, or spacious, as yours. And after all the trouble he's taken to clear the stink of rumor from his name, the last thing the mon needs is Archie and me reviving the odor. Which is why we are moving in here. Archie is establishing himself in London."

This was welcome news to Rory. "Excellent. But why must ye establish yourself at my home, and not yer own?"

Archie Carrington, youngest son of Marquess of Aiken, finally spoke for himself. "Haven't got the time, have I? I'm the newest writer for *The Spectator,* and I reckon to come on the town with a splash."

Rory clapped him on the back. "Congratulations, ye scribbling piker."

Archie accepted his friendly insult with a flourishing bow. "Thank ye, ye damned dilettante."

"No longer a mere dilettante," Rory countered. "Have ye not heard that I am now the principal authority—a *connoisseur,* if ye please—in the Old Masters at Mr. Christie's Auction Houses?"

"Who'd have ever predicted all that study would have rubbed off on ye," Archie joked.

"I did." Alasdair, young Member of Parliament, and the most ambitiously serious of the four—which was also why he had most successfully scrubbed the Scots from his accent—brought the teasing to a halt. "I predicted it years ago. Which is exactly why we have come to see you."

A lovely low hum of anticipation tightened in Rory's chest. "Is one of ye in trouble?" Because trouble was what he liked best—trouble was his middle name.

Actually, his middle name was Andrew, but if re-consulted on the choice, even his father would admit that

Trouble would have been a more appropriate name for his ramshackle by-blow of a youngest son.

And trouble—the ability to get in and out of it with equal felicity—was why he had made such steadfast friends, and what had brought them all to London. Rory was eager to try his hand again after their last episode—a malignant tide of false rumor and damning innuendo that had nearly pulled poor staid, upright Alasdair under, and which had resulted in their relocation from Edinburgh to London— had been concluded in such satisfactory fashion with Alasdair's bruised reputation not only repaired, but burnished to a smart town gloss.

"Not trouble," Ewan, the most cautious of their group, hedged. "We're not actually sure, yet. At least, I'm not sure."

"I'm sure." Archie contradicted. "I've got a nose for this sort of thing."

From the other side of the room Alasdair made a rude sound. "But not the brain."

"It's not the brain I'm lacking, but the eyes. And the fingers," Archie countered. "Rory has both. Always has."

Rory tried to make light of his less than savory skills, learned well before he had ever met his friends. "Ye're just jealous of my gloriously mis-spent youth."

"No. We just want to put that well-spent youth to good use," Alasdair said flatly. "For the good of your friends."

Alasdair knew just how to appeal to him. Loyalty to these three men was the beginning and end of who Rory was as a man. They'd been through thick and thin together, these lads and he. Mostly thick. As sons of Scots peers, the four of them had been shipped off to school in France to acquire airs and graces befitting their status, though Rory always thought his father had shipped him off to keep his embarrassment of a by-blow out of the way. But through school, and then through university at St. Andrews—where they had raised considerable hell—his friends had never once seemed to care that he was a bastard, never treated him as lesser, and in so doing had cemented his lifelong devotion to them.

But he would be more devoted to them once he had coffee. "Breakfast first, trouble after."

"As much as I would love to laze about all the morning like you fine *gentlemen*," Alasdair gave the word a wry intonation, "I have to get back to the Home Office, where I have important work to do. So I should like to sort out this little matter of a potential crime before I do."

"Potential crime?" The pleasurable tingling of excitement spread from his chest to his fingertips. To keep from drumming his fingers against the table in anticipation, Rory busied himself by filling his cup and taking a scalding sip. "Tell me all."

"As I'm sure you know," Alasdair began, "things are all-hands-to-the-whip in the art market these days, with all these dispossessed French aristos setting up house in London with nothing to show for hundreds of years of life in the nobility but a Holbein or Titian salvaged from the family chateau."

"Yes." This was not news to Rory. "I've been making a very good living out of helping them turn such artistic assets into cold hard cash with the help of good Mr. Christie. We had a particularly successful auction just last night."

"We know. We were there. Oh, you were working so diligently we didn't like to bother you," Alasdair explained. "But we were there because Ewan spotted something that gave me pause. This one painting"—Alasdair held out a dogeared copy of the sale catalogue—"listed as *Girl with a Guitar* by Vermeer, sounded a great deal too like that gem of a Vermeer that sits next to the chimney piece in Ewan's study at Crieff."

Rory had seen the painting only last night—even though it was an Old Master, and his area of expertise, his employer, Mr. James Christie had personally handled the consignment. But he had not seen, nor heard, anything to alarm in the sale. "Vermeer often painted these drolleries, or genre paintings. Ewan's subject has a lute. This one has a guitar." He put his feet up on Alasdair's chair, just to bother him. "I still cannot find within your narrative sufficient motive for ye to violate the sanctity of my breakfast room before noon."

"But…" Archie looked to Ewan.

Ewan obliged him with an explanation. "But my father bought the painting—many years ago, ye understand—from the same family collection that is selling this other Vermeer, now."

"And I thought 'Who buys two Vermeers of almost exactly the same subject?'" Alasdair brought the discussion back under his control. "Because it seems very much like the case that got you started."

"Ah." Rory had indeed 'got started' in his present career by a similar circumstance. He had studied art, both at school in France and at university in Scotland, and as a result he had been tasked by his father, the Earl, with cataloguing the family art collection. Whereupon he had found discrepancies, and uncovered at least two very old, very well-made forgeries that had been sold into his father's collection as being by the famed French portraitist François Clouet. In doing so, he had made a name for himself as something of an expert in the detection and uncovering of forged masterpieces—it had less to do with an artistic 'eye' than with an eye for details and discrepancies in the paperwork.

"And so we went to see it, the three of us," Alasdair went on. "And the painting hanging on the wall at Mr. Christie's is remarkably similar to Ewan's."

"Remarkably." Ewan confirmed. "And what makes it remarkable, is that my father bought that painting from the Comte du Blois himself, back in '78."

"And," Archie was quick to add. "The piece was put up for sale by the current head of the house of Blois, the old count's rapscallion nephew."

"Charles Blois." Rory looked from one to the other, and felt his smile widen—he had a bit of a soft spot for rapscallion youngest sons. "Who studied painting in his youth. Who in the short time he has been in London, has sold paintings into at least half of the important collections in England. Who has been everything discreet and above board." Rory felt that glorious tingle paint straight down his spine. "And whom I suspect *you* suspect of forgery."

"Yes." Alasdair was characteristically to the point. "And from the point of view of the Home Office, we can't have *that* in London."

"Of course not." For his own part, Rory was rather glad they had 'that' in London—he'd have no work otherwise.

"And what's more"—Alasdair was not done—"we can't have someone forging our Ewan's paintings. It simply won't do."

And that was why he loved these men—loyalty. "It won't."

"No," Archie agreed. "And I talked to him as well, Charles Blois, and he was more than happy to tell me about a Hals also in his possession, that sounded entirely fishy to us."

"And just imagine," Alasdair went on in his magnetic way, "if you could expose a living, breathing, money-making forger in the heart of the London art market. Your career would be made."

"And so would mine," Archie added. "Because I'm going to write all about it."

The tingle shot right up Rory's spine like a bolt. Because Rory could imagine it. He could imagine what it would be like to finally gain the full admiration his lack of birthright had denied him. He could imagine it all. "We'll set a thief to catch a thief."

"I like the sound of that." Alasdair rubbed his hands together and smiled.

"I think this calls for brandy for breakfast." Rory retrieved the decanter, and turned to survey his friends. "I hope ye packed evening clothes, gents. If ye're coming to live with me, ye'll need to cut quite a dash."

Chapter 3

MIGNON SAVED HER breath to cool her porridge, as the English were wont to say. Because outside the window, Soho Square filled with the sound of a great commotion.

Mignon peeked down from the dormer to see a great coach wheel up to the house with armed outriders. Her chest filled with the cold clutch of dread. This was how their flight had started in Paris—with riders at the door. "Papa, there are riders! They have come to arrest you!"

"Who?" He scrambled to the window to peer out before she could pull him back. "Oh, Mignon." He relaxed against the window frame. "What a shock you gave me. It is only Sir Joshua Reynolds come to talk to me of the Verrocchio Diana."

The cold dread cooled to chilly alarm. "What of the Verrocchio?" The statue had been the most important piece of art that they had taken from France. *She* had taken, actually—she had snatched the foot-tall marble statue to use as a weapon as they had run from the house. But today the Diana had pride of place, both in Papa's collection, and in his heart. Because it was also a forgery—one that his own papa had made.

Like father, like son—scoundrels all.

And the scoundrel was in the midst of one of his

schemes. "Sir Joshua asks for the Diana statue to be the centerpiece of a great collection of masterpieces to be exhibited by the Royal Academy of Arts at Somerset House."

"Oh, no. Absolutely not." Such a plan was potentially worse than if Papa had been arrested—it would only encourage him to paint more by feeding his vanity and pride.

"Why not? Why should it not be shared? It is a great masterpiece."

"Papa, you should not even let it from the house."

"No, no. The time has come. The Diana must be seen." He threw off his smock and went to the basin, where he scrubbed his paint-splattered hands before heading for the door through the armoire. "Don't fuss."

She would do more than fuss—she had to make him think more clearly. "I beg you listen to me. This is madness. You were the one who insisted—"

"*Non*," he insisted. "I must go to the man—he has come in all this state." Once on the other side of the passage through the *armoire*, Papa donned a deeply embroidered court coat that was still magnificent, even if it were a little threadbare. "And my shoes—where are my heeled shoes?"

Against her better judgement, she handed him the shoes. "Papa, they are here."

"Think of it, my angel—with this money from the sale, I can hire a valet, and you will no longer have to fetch my shoes."

"Think very carefully before you do, Papa. That will mean another person who knows your secret. Or another person from whom you must keep it." Oh, what a tangled web. "I beg you to reconsider."

"You worry too much, Mignon! Just like your mother, God keep her. Do I smell of paint?" He took up an atomizer of *eau de cologne*, and sprayed himself liberally.

Too liberally—Mignon could barely breathe for the thick mist of scent. "Papa." She waved the air around her face. "You must stop and think. The Diana is a forgery."

"*Chut.*" He made an abrupt sound of rebuke. "That is a word I cannot abide. It is a beautiful work of art."

"A beautiful work of art that was not sculpted by Verrocchio." She stood her ground, barring his way.

He simply put his hands on her tiny waist and moved her bodily. "Come, you will like Sir Joshua," he cajoled. "He is impeccably honest, and therefore entirely dull. I insist, even though you are dressed in this dull English manner—you look like a shepherdess."

Mignon saved her arguments about fashion for another day, and dutifully followed him down the stair, thought she was reluctant to become any part of Papa's charade.

"My dear Sir Joshua." Papa's greeting of the head of the Royal Academy was everything effusive. "How kind of you to come in person."

Sir Joshua Reynolds made her father a cordial bow. "My pleasure, I assure you, Count Blois."

The title was another falsity Papa had adopted on the death of his cousin, the *Comte du Blois.*

"Allow me to present my daughter, Marie Chantal." Papa pulled Mignon down the last of the stair.

"Delighted, Mamselle." Sir Joshua made her a courtly, if stiff leg.

With the introduction done, Papa directed their attention to the salon. "Henri, the doors."

Henri dutifully threw back the doors of the salon, where the statue of Diana the Huntress was displayed like a grail atop an altar on the central table.

"There she is." The president of the Royal Academy of Arts clasped his hand to his chest in a show of reverence.

Mignon would just as soon not watch such goings on, but Papa was determined to keep her dutifully at his side. With Mignon in hand, he led the way into the salon. "Allow me, Sir Joshua."

"My dear sir." The Royal Academician was all appreciation. "I first saw her many years ago, on my grand tour. I have never forgotten."

"Oh, yes?" Papa smiled, but Mignon saw the smudge of

heat tinting his cheek— this was a circumstance he had not foreseen. But still, even on the verge of being found out, her scoundrel of a papa looked only vaguely uneasy.

Mignon thought she was going to be ill.

"Yes." Sir Joshua was walking around the plinth. "I was fortunate enough to see this at the Hotel de Blois in Paris."

Papa passed his hand over his eyes. "Happier times, *monsieur*. Much happier times."

"I am so sorry for the loss of your family, of your cousin, the count." Sir Joshua bowed his head in condolence. "The tales one hears from France these days… So dreadful."

"Thank you. Such tales leave me *désolé*, my dear Sir Joshua. Absolutely desolate." Papa closed his eyes, and shook his head. "But I have my Mignon, and we are here, alive and well in London, with our Verrocchio, which we were fortunate enough to save."

Sir Joshua could not be effusive enough in his praise. "Sublime, I said then, and sublime I say now. I express my gratitude, not only for myself, but also on behalf of the Royal Academy. Thank you for letting loaning us the Diana as the centerpiece of this exhibition to raise funds for those who find themselves refugees from the terror."

Papa was everything modest, and subdued, and false. "It is my honor to do so much for my countrymen. I only wish I could do more."

Sir Joshua Reynolds signaled to the small army of attendants lining the foyer—who knew Soho Square rated such precautions—to bring in a special crate. Clearly they did not want the Diana stolen, or damaged.

Which gave her an entirely new idea—if she could not stop this farce with logic, perhaps she could with mishap. "Let me help you, Papa." She reached for the figurine.

But her papa had not escaped the mob just to be outwitted by her. "Oh, no, no." He cut her off, and wrapping the Diana in his silk handkerchief, he removed the stone goddess from the plinth himself.

Mignon tried again. "Papa, let me help you. Let me take the base—"

"No, no," he cried again. "You may touch it only with gloved hands. The oils from your skin, my dear—they will stain the marble." He turned to the academician. "Into your hands, Sir Joshua, I give you this, our ultimate treasure. Care for it as if it were your very own."

Sir Joshua hastily donned his gloves, and very carefully passed the statue into the gloved hands of the attendants, who placed the Diana carefully into the straw-lined wooden traveling crate.

Mignon tried again, for she might still prevent the forgery from being exhibited if she dropped and broke the marble base.

But she was hopelessly outclassed—Papa's wiles were of an altogether higher order than hers would ever be. "Mignon!" He snatched the base from her hands. "Have a care, my dear. There." He handed the base to the footman to pack away with the rest of the statue.

There was nothing Mignon could do but watch as the statue was crated up and carried out of the house to the coach as if it were a queen lying in state. And then Sir Joshua was making his goodbyes, and the groomsmen were mounted, and the whole troupe jangled off down the street, bound for Somerset House. And the public display of a forgery.

"Oh, Papa. I wish I did not have the most awful feeling of foreboding. The same terrible feeling of dread as that awful week before we left France."

Her papa would not be drawn by either sentimentalism or fatalism. "But it was a good thing we left France, a great thing. Look at this house." He flourished his arm like a conjurer. "We never lived like this in Paris."

"You were not selling forged paintings like hot horse chestnuts in Paris."

"Ah, where is your *esprit de crops*, your spirit of adventure?"

But it was a rhetorical question, because both of them knew exactly where her *esprit* had gone—left behind in Paris where it belonged.

"These forgeries are our security in uncertain times," Papa insisted. "What if something should happen to me, and there was no money? What would you do—become a seamstress?" He answered his own question. "No! Better to sell a painting. Or loan out a statue."

"Oh, Papa, I wish I could make you understand what you are doing is wrong."

He made one of his many sounds of Gallic dismissal. "Don't look at me like that. The loan of the statue is necessary to enhance the reputation of the Blois collection, so the world will know that *Comte* Charles Blois escaped France with coaches filled with treasures that I may be persuaded to part with in good time, due to the unfortunate fact that I am separated from the family estates, perhaps forever, by the revolution. I have lost my family, but I still have my treasures. A treasure like the Verrocchio Diana."

"Except that it's not by Verrocchio."

"Why must you talk like that? It is art! Brilliant art. Why must you be so negative?"

"I worry, Papa. These Englishmen, they are great collectors, difficult to fool."

"*You* have become too English, with your need for precision, and your worry, worry, worry."

"You may make light of my worry, but one day, Papa, you will overstep. One of your forgeries you will sell to the wrong man."

He dismissed such a possibility. "Who? Who will be able to tell? Who knows more than I?" He answered his own questions. "No one. No, they cannot tell, these Englishmen. They are all too happy to snap up our patrimony at what they think are bargain prices. Well, I have bargains for them. And when I think of the money I have turned down already for the Verrocchio, it gives me palpitations. Why, at the auction of my Vermeer, I was offered ten thousand pounds. Guineas! A fortune."

"Papa. It. Is. A. Crime."

"*Chut.* The problem with you is you're too honest—a rogue branch off the family tree. I blame your mother, God rest her soul. Oh, I don't say that to hurt you, my child." Papa came to sit beside her and pat her hand. "You cannot help what you are."

"Thank you, Papa."

"What you need is a sherry." He moved toward the drinks tray. "I will have *cognac* to celebrate, but you are too English, and ought best have sherry." He brought her a healthy measure of the nut-brown fortified wine. "Oh, my darling. You must see that I am proud that our Verrocchio is a forgery. It is nothing to make something from one's imagination—but to copy or create in the style of a genius, stroke for stroke, line for line, chisel mark, by chisel mark— that takes something more than genius."

Mignon had heard similar lectures before, but never with quite so much gusto.

The rich wine seared its way down her dry throat as Papa went on. And on. "Be proud that your own grandfather had the cunning and eye to sculpt it, and your own grandmother the beauty and poise and scandalous nature to pose for it. For months she stood naked, without moving a muscle. My uncle and cousin were scandalized, of course—they had not the true Blois sensibility. But my cousin is gone now—they are all gone. And we will do what we must to see the name of Blois restored, and celebrated." He smiled at her in his scoundrel way. "You must put on your prettiest French frock, and come to the exhibition's opening." He sighed with anticipatory contentment. "I do so like a party."

Chapter 4

MIGNON DID NOT put on a *robe à la française*, nor did she go with papa to the soirée at Somerset House—he might have taken her presence for approval, or worse, encouragement. Instead, she took the opportunity to give Henri and Madame Henri, who was their cook, the evening free for themselves, while she curled up in front of a bright cozy fire with the latest novel.

All was quiet and bliss until something, somewhere in the house, went bump forcefully enough to make Mignon jump. Pricks of fear needled under her skin—this is how it had started in Paris—a thump at the door, then a brick through the window.

Mignon held her breath, listening intently, trying to sort out the normal background sounds of the city outside the window from the product of her frantic imagination. She had almost convinced herself that there was nothing when she heard the second unmistakable sound of furniture crashing onto the parquet floor of the salon.

Fear chilled her skin like a rime of ice, but still she tried to rationalize away the spreading dread—Papa must have gotten back early, and without Henri to light all the lamps, might have stumbled into the furniture. That's all it was. Surely.

Still, her heart rattled in her chest like an ice-covered shutter.

But she could not sit in her warm room quaking in cowardly terror—Papa might be hurt. He might need her. Perhaps he had imbibed too much champagne, and needed assistance coming up the stairs. It wasn't like him to become cup-shot, but stranger things had happened.

And stranger things were at that moment happening, because half way down the darkened stair the draft from a wide open window chilled her to the bone, filling her with more than dread. Because she knew she had not left a window open so wide that the curtains fluttered and danced like nervous ghosts, or made the single taper Henri had left at the bottom of the stair waver and shake like her knees, knocking together in abject terror.

Because in that wavering light, she saw the long spectral shadow of a man wielding a small beam of light, searching the walls of the salon. For art. Forged art.

Mignon's legs collapsed under her, and the old staircase creaked under her weight.

The light in the salon abruptly went out.

She clapped her hand over her mouth to keep from the moan of fear forming in the back of her throat from escaping. She froze, cowering on the stair with her chest squeezed tight from trying not to breathe.

After a long moment the light was unshuttered, and the tall shadow began to pry a painting off the wall. And not just any painting, but the Hals *Cavalier* her father had just finished and hung.

Of all the pieces he might have chosen.

What was she to do? It was a long run past the open salon to the front door, and once out in Soho Square she might not be able to raise the watch. But she had to do *something*.

The cold palm she had clamped across her mouth reminded her that her hands were empty—she was unarmed against the intruder. But above her head was a large red baize decorative display of arms—Papa had arranged it adorning the stairwell to remind himself of the armorial displays exhibited at the Blois family chateau of his youth.

It might be a display, but the weapons were actual guns and swords, even if they were ancient. And a weapon in the hand was better than none at all. And if she were very clever, and very quiet, she might just be able to prise one of the small arms—

The first gun would not come away, nor would the second above it. But the long wooden handle of a halberd, with its sharp pike and gleaming axe blade, came off its pegs, sliding silently down to fill her hands.

Thus armed, she drew in a deep breath to steady herself, and to gather enough courage to move. To get up off the stair, and creep nearer to the salon, where the low glow from the fireplace embers revealed the thief closely examining the Hals with the light from his shuttered lantern.

"*Arettez*. Do not move," she said, her voice over-loud and cracked with the fear that gripped her as tightly as she gripped the heavy medieval weapon.

The thief of course moved—whirling around, wielding his lamp to try to find her in the darkness, finally training the thin beam of the lantern on her. "Well damn my eyes," he said in the most pleasant of English tones. "Look at ye."

It was not exactly the sort of response she had been seeking. She moved the head of the weapon to shield her eyes from the light. "Put down that painting." She made her voice firmer. "Put it down. And the lantern as well."

Astonishingly, he did as she bade. Which emboldened her to step sideways, nearer to the bell pull just inside the wide door to the salon—Henri might be out of the house, but the thief might not know that.

Despite the dim lighting, the thief had clearly followed her gaze, and deduced her intent. "Miss Blois, please." The thief smiled as he took two steps toward her. "I can expla—"

"Stay where you are. How do you know my name?" Her voice was high and frightened, but she brandished the halberd with such erratic force that he stopped, and put his hands in the air for good measure.

Yet his voice was everything calm and unruffled. "It's my business to know."

The words themselves chilled her, but his manner—so civil, so helpful, so *English*—took away a great deal of their ice.

From its place against the table, the *Cavalier* smirked up at her. Why the thief could not have set his eye to stealing any of the other paintings—one of the few originals in the premises, for instance—was beyond her. Because this one, she had to defend. She couldn't possibly let it out of the house—the paint was probably not even properly dry. "Why did you choose that painting when you might have taken"— she pointed her pike around the room—"any of the others?"

The thief shrugged, and spread his long lean arms in a gesture of complete innocence. "It was the handiest," he lied cheerfully, ignoring the six other paintings that were closer to the window. "But I'll just go, shall I? No painting, no crime." He smiled charmingly, making polite conversation as if he were at a tea room, and not being held at the business end of a pike. "I was only going to take the one painting, and ye've got so many," he said, as if this justified his crime. "Chances were, ye might not even have missed it."

Clearly he did not know her papa if he thought Charles Blois would not miss even one of his creations. But—

Another idea intruded. "Did my papa put you up to this?" It would be just like her papa to mastermind a theft of his own painting to increase the notoriety of the Blois Collection, as he called his mishmash of stolen family art and forgeries.

"Yer papa?" His eyes narrowed, as if he thought he might have mis-heard her.

Mignon didn't answer his question, nor did she repeat hers. Mostly because she really had to concentrate to keep the long halberd steady in her shaking hands.

"I'll just put the painting back, shall I?" The thief hefted the large frame, and replaced in onto its hooks in the wall. "There." He stepped back to admire it, and then adjusted it, as if it actually mattered to him that it was hung evenly. "Oh, it is magnificent. Pity."

"Pity? About what?"

"Nothing." And then he smiled at her in a way that was meant to show her that he was a rather handsome man—tall and elegantly-formed in a rangy way, with a sweep of curling, sandy hair, and interesting, vivid blue eyes.

She would take it up with *le bon Dieu* at some time later— after God had graciously delivered her of this ruffian—that he should be so capricious as to make a terrible man so light and beautiful. So English, with his lean, intelligent face and long, aristocratic nose.

Which was a strange thing to say about a common housebreaker one was holding at the point of a pike. Which seemed not to be having quite the menacing effect she had intended. Perhaps she needed some show of strength.

Her eyes slid back to the bell pull.

"Ye needn't bother." He had followed her glance. "There's no one there, is there? The house is empty. Except for ye, of course. But it was supposed to be empty while ye were all at the opening of the exhibition."

His casual frankness—not to mention his cheek—was astonishing. "How did you know this?"

"It is my business to know," he repeated. "But I clearly didn't know enough—I didn't know ye'd be here." He cocked his head to the side as if he were trying to see her better. "I'm sorry if I frightened ye out of bed."

Mignon suddenly felt the stupidity of standing there in her thin white night gown, talking to a housebreaker—it was dashed difficult to look intimidating in linen so old it was worn to a transparent softness that was far too revealing.

She felt entirely exposed—the air of the salon prickled against her flesh despite the warmth from the fireplace, and she had to swallow over her dry mouth to say something, anything that would help her feel less vulnerable.

But it was her gentlemanly thief who filled in the

conversational gap. "I thought ye'd be at the opening with your father, ye see. Such a big event like that." He chatted on, as if they were having a pleasant coze over tea, and not over a medieval bladed weapon. "Ye frightened me, too, ye ken. So we're even."

Good Lord, but for an Englishman, he had altogether too much *sang froid.*

Mignon forced herself to find her voice. "I am not frightened. I am angry." She firmed her hands on the handle. "How dare you break into our house."

"I am sorry," he said again. But he didn't look sorry at all—he was smiling at her in a way that made her think that she amused him far more than she intimidated. "But there's really no need for threats of violence. Though ye don't really look as if ye could stab me anyway."

"Of course I could. If I wanted to."

Which she did not want. Not at all. She only wanted to defend herself, and the painting, and be left in peace.

But that brought up another consideration. "Oh, dear God. Are you armed?" she cried. She backed up a few paces herself, because her arms were quivering like the thin birch trees out in the square.

"Heavens, no. I'm a gentleman." He held open the lapels of his well-tailored coat—these English tailors had a way with cutting—to prove he had no weapon.

"A gentleman?" She let her disbelief and disdain color her tone.

"Of sorts—a gentleman thief." He gave her that disarming smile again—the one that was clearly meant to make her go weak at the knees. "But still a gentleman. So as a gentleman, I'd like to ask ye if perhaps ye might put that thing down, or at least aim it a bit less directly as me." His glance slid to the tip of the weapon. "It makes me a trifle nervous."

"Good." She brandished the halberd more firmly. "You are supposed to be more than a trifle nervous."

"Well, that's the criminal class for ye—no proper feelings," he said with breezy insouciance as he gave her another smile, all dazzling apology and glossy charm.

So charming, so English.

She needed to end this episode before she found herself serving him tea and biscuits. "Well, since you have acted almost like a gentleman, then I suppose I might let you go." She favored him with what she hoped was a haughty, superior look to hurry him along. Because the halberd was growing intolerably heavy—her wrists ached.

"Thank ye." He almost bowed, all gracious acceptance of her generosity. "I'll just go the way I came, shall I?"

She was all gracious condescension. "Please."

"Lovely. Don't mind if I do." He rested one long booted leg on the window ledge. "And I must say, ye've been an absolute sport."

And then he winked at her.

"Sport?" The cheek of the man. "Get out," she ordered.

He swung his leg over the sill, his imminent departure assured.

Relief sagged through Mignon with such swiftness that she not only let down her guard, but dropped it entirely, like a fireplace coal. She intended to raise the halberd, and prop it against the wall. Instead, the heavy weapon slipped from her numb fingers, and the tall blade tottered over, like a tree slowly falling in a forest.

And headed directly for the back of her gentleman thief's sandy, English head.

Chapter 5

RORY WENT DOWN so hard, the wind was knocked clean out of him. His ears rang and his lungs burned with the need to breathe, but all other sensation was soon drowned out by the searing ache that swamped him like a bucket of scalding water—a great big wallop of heat and misery emanating from the back of his head.

He instinctively grabbed his skull, as if he would contain the pain. But it was impossible—he was quite literally stupefied.

Eight feet away, Miss Blois looked just as dazed. She stood with her hand over her mouth, looking just as astonished, but utterly horrified at what she had done.

Rory pushed himself upright against the short wall under the window, and tried to take stock. Blood was seeping out of his head and soaking his collar. "Well," he said to no one in particular. "Turns out ye were willing to strike me after all."

Not only willing, but capable. He never would have thought.

Neither, it seemed, did she. "I did not mean to," she protested with a voice as sweet and innocent as a Christmas pudding, as if she had never had any thought in the world of cracking his skull.

"And yet ye did." Rory gingerly felt for the cut on his scalp, and came away with a hand stained red with blood.

Which was not at all a good idea, because at the sight of so much blood, the edges of his vision crowded in, and the world narrowed itself down to the small piece of parquet upon which he sat, stunned and dizzy, and perhaps even dying, judging from the amount of warm stickiness that poured down his neck.

But if he had to go, he supposed he didn't mind being done in by the elfin Miss Blois, because the truth was he had been half-way to heaven the moment he had laid eyes upon her, looming up at him in her night gown, like the ghost of bed partners past.

Or more hopefully, like the ghost of bed partners yet to come.

Either way, he felt decidedly weak at the knees.

Strangely enough, it was tiny Miss Blois who brought him back, patting his cheek, and fanning him in the face with the helpfully transparent skirts of her linen sleeping gown, all modesty forgotten in the crisis.

"*Assez de* bêtises," she said in her native tongue, thinking he wouldn't understand that her tart instruction to end his foolishness was belied by her worried tone. "You cannot be allowed this unbecoming faint," she said in ever-so-slightly-accented English. "You're a burglar—show some fortitude."

"I've got plenty of fortitude," he muttered. "I'm the one who's bleeding."

"Yes, I am sorry. I did not mean at all to hit you. I was trying to put the halberd away."

"Slipshod weapons work, Miss Blois. Ye'd never make it in the army."

"Of a surety, Monsieur Thief." She plied the inside of his wrist to feel his pulse, all helpful, competent nurse—another thing he would not have thought her. "I would not know about such things, not being a gentleman—even a gentleman thief."

"I really don't know about such things, either." He was rambling in his near delirium. "They don't let thieves into the army—gentleman or not."

She almost smiled before she stood, and reached for his arm. "*Allors*, we must have you up before you bleed onto the carpets."

"Yer pardon, Miss Blois." He let her assist him off the floor.

Up close, she was even smaller, and more adorably attractive, fussing at him in such a bossy, concerned way. And if she would let him lean on her, he was sure he could find a way to see down the front of her marvelously translucent gown. "I'm afraid I'm going to need something to staunch the flow. Head wounds bleed terribly, don't ye know."

"I do not know." She was all practical necessity. "Can you stand alone? There are some bandages in the kitchens, in *Madame*'s pantry. Here, let me assist you."

Even though she probably weighed less than a hundredweight, and wouldn't even come up to his collarbone, she slipped her arms around his waist, and heaved him up, like a stevedore shouldering a bale. She had altogether too much strength and self-possession for a wisp of a lass in a night gown.

He had best be on his guard. "Ye won't whack me again, will ye?"

She proved immune to his charm. "Of a certainty, I might. So mind yourself."

"Yes, ma'am." He slung his arm across her shoulder, and leaned gently onto her delicate strength. Which also let him sample the soft slide of skin along the back of her neck. If she made a fuss at such a liberty, he could cry delirium. Because he was feeling delightfully lightheaded.

But she didn't protest. Not too much, anyway—she took the wrist he slung across her shoulder in a gingerly sort of way, until he could take a hand rail to steady himself on the kitchen stair.

"Sit there." When they reached the kitchen, she pointed to a chair at the head of a short deal table. "And take that beautiful coat off before it is ruined utterly. I hope you have a good laundress who knows how to deal with such bloodstains. Cold water, you must tell her. And a solution of hydrogen water."

Rory's guard finally came slamming down like a rusty portcullis—it was a rare lass who had a working knowledge of chemistry. Perhaps Miss Mignon Blois was not as fey and innocent as she looked. "I'll tell her."

Miss Blois very quickly proceeded to the business at hand, laying out bandages from some sort of medical cabinet, and proceeding to open bottles of noxious smelling medicines.

"What is that?" He didn't want to seem fussy, but a fellow ought to be cautious about what he allowed in, or on, his body. It was a general rule he'd adopted during his school years—when all sorts of culinary indignities had been forced upon him—and strived to follow ever since.

"A styptic," she said, as if that would answer everything. "Certain things mixed with brandy. It will stop the bleeding."

A sound plan. Roy shucked himself out of his dark evening coat, and found the collar soaked with blood. "A field apothecary, are ye?"

Miss Blois stuck one hand on her very trim hip, and pointed with the other to the kitchen door, as if to tell him he was welcome to leave at any time—the choice was his. "Stop your complaint and lean your head over, nearer the light." She moved a lamp closer to take a better look at the laceration on his head. "It is not so very bad."

"No? Ye made a rather thorough job of it for an amateur." He eyed her dark bottles. "Will it hurt?"

"Probably." She pursed her rather wonderfully full lips, and considered him with one raised eyebrow. "For a burglar, you are not so very brave."

"I'm a society burglar. I didn't expect someone of yer elevated class to be so bloodthirsty as to actually wound me."

"I am not in the least elevated. Nor bloodthirsty." Yet, she took her revenge for this perceived insult by slapping the stinging styptic to his scalp.

"Och! For the love of—" he crowed. And slapped his hand down on top of hers, trapping her there. Mostly for the chance to feel the lovely, soft, smooth skin of her delicate hands—deceptively soft and sweet, even if they had proved rather deadly. But he would play-act writhing pain if it meant he could touch her again.

Damn his eyes, but she was lovelier each look he took. And she smelled divine—like a Provençal garden, all fresh sea air and bright florals.

She was having none of it. "Such drama. You carry on like the veriest baby," she chided in her French way. "It is only the small cut to your flesh."

"Well, it's my flesh that is cut." He shaded his voice with reproach.

"You must expect some occupational hazard when you are a thief," she observed tartly. "Gentleman or not, you broke in here to steal."

Not exactly, but it were best if she didn't know what he had planned for that Hals. "Ye are of course in the right, while I am very firmly in the wrong. It is undoubtedly a hazard of my occupation, and must been borne with a stiff upper lip."

"Stiff upper lip?" She stepped away to take a long look at him. And what she saw must have pleased her at least a little, because she almost smiled—a bemused pout of her plush lower lip. "You are a very English sort of burglar."

It was everything he could do to keep himself from laughing. "Had many burglars, have ye?"

"No," she admitted philosophically. "You are the first."

He gifted her with his most gentlemanly, charming smile—the one that had melted hearts from Edinburgh's Royal Mile all the way to Paris' *Montmartre*. "I'm honored."

She remained impervious. "Do not be." The tartness was back. "Hold still." She ran her fingers carefully through his hair, parting it so she could sluice warm water against the wound. "It is very small—a nothing. There will be the merest scar."

She pressed a clean cloth to his head. But then he felt her fingers still stroking gently through his hair, though there was no longer a reason. "It is very strange, your hair. It is the color of ripened wheat."

While Rory had often heard himself described as strange, he could not help but be flattered. It was an un-looked for intimacy, this light touch of her fingertips against his hair. He wanted to close his eyes, and lean into her small palm and rest, if only for a moment or two before he had to return to the world outside her lovely warm kitchen.

She said nothing more, but made a delicious soft sound of concentration while she dressed the wound with an aromatic salve, and wrapped what felt like a mile of bandage around his head. But he didn't mind. He took the opportunity to settle more of his weight onto the delicate strength of her torso, and inhale a lungful of her subtle scent.

It was a bliss stronger than brandy.

"The French would say to air this wound of yours in a day or two by taking off the bandages, but I know you English have other, equally beneficial practices. If you are concerned, perhaps you should have an apothecary check it in a day or two."

"If I don't know which practices are the most beneficial," he admitted cheerfully, "it's only because I've never taken a halberd to my head before."

She drew back to survey her handiwork. "*Ça suffit*—that will do, as you English say. And now it is past time for you to go." She pointed at the kitchen door. "I should not want any of the others to come home and find a criminal in the kitchens."

He lavished her with his best smile. "Did ye have a better spot in mind?"

She did not appreciate his crooked sense of humor. She gave him what he could only describe as a French look—all arched eyebrows and pursed lips. "You, *Monsieur* Gentleman Thief, are altogether too cheeky."

"Yer pardon, *Mademoiselle.*" He gave her his best

continental pronunciation. "I'll go." He stood and carefully slid his arms into his ruined coat—his tailor was going to have a fit. But it had been worth the price. "Ye've been most understanding." He bowed again more formally once he had himself to a reasonable resemblance of rights.

But bowing made his head swim, and he staggered.

"What is wrong?" She instinctively came to his aid, wrapping her arm around his waist, and propping him up against the kitchen wall.

He took advantage of the intimacy to loop one of his own arms about her neck, and lean on her, rather than the wall. "I feel weak," he lied. "From the blood loss."

But tiny Miss Blois was made of sturdier stuff than to meekly fall for his gammon. She made a subtly derisive tssking noise with her lips. "Come now. You hardly bled at all considering—the wound is small. It did more damage to your suit of clothes than to your hard head."

He nevertheless did not relinquish her support. "I am weak on behalf of my tailor."

She managed to extract herself from his embrace with a neat twist. "You are weak in the head, with or without a wound. Go." She pointed at the kitchen door.

What a charming, picturesque figure she made in her bare feet and translucent sleeping gown and luminous eyes the color of the pale moon.

"But I can't ride like this," he protested, trying to do anything to prolong the unique intimacy of the encounter. "What if I fall off my horse and crack my head open?"

She shrugged in that supremely French way—all knowing unconcern. "Some enterprising urchin would pick your pockets, sell your hair and your teeth to the apothecary, and your clothes to the rag traders, and then, whatever was left of your body"—and here she tipped her head to the side as if appraising his body very carefully indeed—"would very likely be sold to the anatomy surgeons."

"Good God." He could only laugh, though her dismal scenario was all too likely. "Ye French certainly are a bloodthirsty lot."

Everything charming and accommodating within her changed in that instant—her face went as blank and still as an empty canvas. "Do not speak to me of things you cannot possibly know." She picked up a wooden rolling pin, and even if she did not actually brandish it at him, she made her point. "Go."

"My apology, *Mademoiselle*." Clearly he had hit upon a rather raw nerve. He should have remembered that it was said that though she and her father had escaped the bloodthirsty mob, the rest of their family had not. "I'm going." He gave in with as much good grace as possible. "I'll walk. And it's not too far should I fall."

"Not too far from here? Where do you live?"

He gave her an approximation of the truth. "Brooks's."

"Brooks's Club?" She looked impressed. Or disgusted—he could not quite tell from her wide-eyed expression. "They must let anyone in."

"They do." He grinned in agreement. "I often say that I don't like being a member of any club that would want me for a member, but that's neither here nor there. It occurs to me, Miss Blois, if the night watchman finds my horse tethered to yer iron fence"—he gestured up the exterior kitchen stairs toward the unseen front of the house—"I can only imagine it might be very bad for yer reputation."

She gaped at him. "You have left a horse? Soho Square is not Paris, but you will be lucky if the animal has not been stolen."

"Oh, I'm always lucky," he assured her.

Miss Blois was not so sanguine. "This from a thief with a hole in his head. Me, I am not so lucky, so go and take this horse of yours from my fence before my reputation in London is tattered to shreds."

"I will take every care with yer reputation."

She tossed up her hands. "This care I need like the hole in your head. You may take your care at a distance, *Monsieur* Thief." Her voice was running as dry as her patience. "Go."

"I'll go." Rory finally put word into action by grasping his laborious way along the wrought iron stair rail. "If I could trouble ye to just see me to my carriage?"

"First it is a horse, and now it is a carriage?"

"I'm confused. Blood loss, ye ken."

She made another soft sound of remonstrance. But she assisted him with a small but steady hand at the small of his back as he grappled his way up the stair. "Oof. You are heavier than you look. Let us pray this horse and carriage of yours is not stolen."

"Serve me right if it were, since I stole it in the first place," he lied cheerfully He hadn't stolen anything in years—tonight's attempt excepted—but he found he liked surprising her.

She gasped just as he had hoped she would. "*Bon Dieu.*"

"Perhaps ye'll be so kind as to unlock the gate for me. In my present state, I don't think I'm capable of picking the lock." He gave her what he hoped was a charming smile. "So much nicer if I don't have to."

"Ooh." She dashed back down the stair on her delightfully little bare feet, and returned from the kitchen presently, clutching the gate key. "There." She pushed the wrought iron gate open wide to see him through, and then absolutely gaped at his canary yellow, high perch phaeton. "Is it not that what you English would call 'a bit flash' for a burglar who ought to be inconspicuous?"

"It's just the thing for getaways," he assured her. "Highly maneuverable. Especially with that pair." He stroked the nose of the nearest of his pair of superb Thoroughbreds.

She assessed the equipage with a critical eye. "This business of being a gentleman thief must be very profitable."

Rory gave her his version of that nonchalant Gallic shrug. "As I said, it's stolen."

She crossed her arms over her chest, giving him an absolutely stunning view of her breasts through the thin lawn of her white sleeping gown—he was as stunned as if he had taken another blow to the head.

It took him a long moment to find his voice. "My dear Miss Blois, if ye insist on presenting yerself to me in this intimate fashion, I'm going to have to give ye my name."

This time he more than surprised her—he utterly astonished her. She gasped, and her plush lower lip fell slack, before she drew back with a hand clutched to her throat. "I cannot marry you, *Monsieur*."

Rory near choked on his laugh. "I beg yer pardon, *Mademoiselle*. I meant no disrespect. I meant only to introduce myself." Even with her lovely breasts distracting him, Rory still had enough presence of mind to lie. "Mr. Andrews," he supplied on the next breath. "Rory Andrews."

She put her hand to her mouth to cover her astonishment. "Why would a thief tell me his name? I might report you—Mr. Andrews of Brooks's Club—to the watch. It is my duty to do so."

"So ye may," he acknowledged. "But I have the strangest feeling—which is entirely rare in my business, I assure ye— that ye're completely trustworthy."

"You are mad." She gaped at him. "Absolutely and completely mad."

He gave her his best smile yet. "All the best burglars are, ye ken. Oh, one more thing I forgot to steal."

And very quickly, he leaned in low, and kissed her lovely, soft, plush, astonished lips. "Thank ye, *chère Mademoiselle Blois*, for a most memorable evening."

Chapter 6

"MIGNON?" PAPA'S VOICE came from the foyer as Mignon sat alone in the kitchen, waiting for her heartbeat to stop clattering in her ears.

"Here, Papa." She rose and headed upstairs. "I'm here."

"Ah, Mignon, my angel." He greeted her with kisses on both cheeks. "What a pity you missed the exhibition. All the *ton*, as they call their society, was there, fawning, dressed from head to toe in silks and satins. Oh, you should have seen it. Our Diana was the center of attention. All the world and his brother was there to see her. A triumph! A triumph, I tell you."

"How nice." She followed him into the salon where he lit a branch of candles, giving the room a warm glow. Warm enough to see a small stain of blood on the parquet next to the still-billowing window.

Mignon crossed to latch the window shut. "Papa, I caught an intruder."

"Of course you did, angel." Papa's mind was too full of success to attend her properly, especially while he poured himself a large cognac. "How like you to do something like that—" His head whipped around. "An intruder? Here?"

"Yes, Papa. A burglar. A thief." Mignon poured herself into a chair before her legs gave out. "An articulate, oh-so-clever, gentleman thief." She had Papa's full attention now, but she felt utterly drained, as if all the tension and nerve that had held her up during the encounter had finally run out.

"Good Lord. You're as pale as your chemise." Papa came to her side, all belated parental concern. "Here, take a sip of this."

Mignon took the snifter he handed her, and gulped the cognac straight down. A warm, reviving fire kindled instantly in her tummy, chasing away her chill. Convincing her that the strange feeling of relief she had felt at Mr. Andrews's departure had not been disappointment—she was glad he was gone. And not even a little sorry that he had been injured.

Well, perhaps a little sorry. His beautiful, well-cut coat *had* been ruined.

Papa refilled her drink from the decanter in his hand. "You must tell me all about it, my poor darling, every detail."

"Well." What could she say? What *should* she say—she never knew how her dear papa was going to take something. "It was pitch dark here in the salon, except for the candle Henri had left in the foyer, and I was alone—Henri and Madame being given the night off, you remember. And there was a noise—I thought it was you, so I came down." She took another, more measured sip of the potent cognac, and pulled what was left of her wits together. "And there he was in the salon—tall, blue eyes the color of a marble, sandy hair, slim in an English, sword-fighter sort of way. Quite good looking, I suppose. If one were looking critically."

Papa was staring at her. "And were you looking critically?"

"Oh, yes. Very critically." She shook the thought right out of her head. "He was a thief, Papa. Even if he called himself a gentleman thief, he was a terrible man. Terrible. Awful. No sense of guilt or shame. Not that that matters to you, of course."

"No, no."

"But he was entirely too easy about the whole affair. Terribly cheeky. No proper feeling at all—he was not in the least ashamed of being a thief, or getting caught, or being wounded."

Papa choked on his cognac. "Wounded!"

"Yes. Well, I hit him over the head with the halberd. Quite by accident, of course, but he had been going to take the Hals."

Now, she *really* had his attention. "The Hals?" Papa shot to his feet, and turned toward his *Cavalier.* "My Hals?"

"Your Hals," she confirmed.

Papa warded off his shock by retrieving the cognac decanter, and pouring them both another medicinal measure. "*Bon Dieu.* Tell me all."

"I took the halberd down to stop him from taking the painting. But it fell on him quite by accident. At least I think it did." It was all a little mixed-up in her mind. "But then once I had wounded him, I did not want to call the watch, as I thought it might lead to all sorts of magistrates and awkward questions about the Hals, and… well, you know, Papa."

"Yes, yes. That might have been very awkward. Magistrates." He closed his eyes, as if the very thought of the robed arm of the law were giving him a fit of nervous apprehension.

Mignon let out the breath she didn't know she had been holding. "That is what I thought, too, so I let him go. Without the Hals."

"Oooh." Papa collapsed into the settee beside her. "What a close run thing. Brave Mignon. I hope your wounding him served him a harsh warning." Papa paused. "He wasn't badly hurt, was he?"

"No, no. Just a scratch, really. I dressed the wound to be sure. But you should have heard him carrying on. Very unprofessional."

"Ah good." Papa looked visibly relieved. "Perhaps he was an amateur? I suppose he must have been one to be so easily caught."

It wasn't as if it had been *easy* to catch him. "Perhaps. But he seemed rather too successful to be an amateur. Though he did say I was the first person who had ever attacked him. He was honored, he said."

"Did he? You seemed to have had a good long chat."

"Yes. It was too awful." But the repeated application of cognac had done its work—she began to feel pleasantly numb. "But now that you are home, and the doors and windows are locked, and everything is safe, I just want to go to bed, and forget it all."

"Of course you do." Papa was staring at the Hals on the wall. "But in your long chat, did this gentleman thief perhaps mention why he was taking the Hals?"

"He said it was the handiest, though of course, it was not. But, Papa?" Something in her father's tone penetrated her pleasant numbness. "What did you say? What did you do?"

"Nothing, nothing. But perhaps I was a little indiscreet at the auction, when my Vermeer was fetching such a ravishing price. But it was a young man with dark hair I was speaking to—nothing as you describe this gentleman thief. Perhaps it was just a coincidence. The handiest painting, as he said."

Perhaps the man had told the truth. Despite the fact that the tall gentleman thief had had to cross the room from the window, and pass at least three other paintings—two of which were not forgeries.

But it was all too hard to figure out with so much good brandy in her belly, clouding her brain. "Goodnight, Papa."

"Good night, my darling." He kissed her cheeks, and sent her toward the stair.

But just as she reached the first step he stopped her. "Darling? This terrible, tall, blue-eyed thief, he didn't molest you in any way?"

"No. No. He was the perfect gentleman. For a thief."

In the end, the only thing he had managed to steal was a kiss.

They were all waiting for him when he returned to his townhouse—Archie, Ewan and Alasdair—lounging about his library, drinking his good brandy as if they owned the place. Alasdair had even gone so far as to seat himself behind Rory's desk.

"Do make yerselves at home," he invited in a tone rife with annoyance.

After so many years of friendship, they were deaf to his sarcasm. It took a long moment before anyone actually looked at him.

"Bloody hell, Rory!" Archie was the least patient of his friends, and nearly levitated himself from his chair. "What in blazes happened?"

What had not happened? "Things were rather more complicated than anticipated."

"Were you caught?" Alasdair gave him one of his wry, half-smiles. "Which would be embarrassing. But not impossible to deal with."

"I didn't get caught, exactly." Rory wasn't sure how much of his tale he wanted to tell—the encounter with Miss Blois didn't exactly show him in the best light.

"Exactly what *did* happen, Cathcart?" Alasdair probed.

"What did ye find out?" Archie was much more broad in his inquiry.

Ewan was more precise. "Did ye get the painting?"

"I did not," Rory admitted. "The lass was there."

"Lass?"

"Oh, no." Alasdair pushed back in his chair. "Everything always goes to hell in a hand cart the minute our Rory starts talking about a lass."

It might have been insulting if it hadn't been true. At least in the past. Miss Blois was…different. "This was a purely professional exchange. Of weapons," he clarified. "She cracked me over the head with a pike. And the least ye lazy layabouts could do under the circumstance is pour me a brandy."

Archie swore another blue streak, but he moved quickly

to fetch the decanter.

"Tell us all," Alasdair urged. "But tell us first if you need a surgeon?"

"No, I thank ye. She patched me up."

"The lass?" Archie handed him a well-filled glass.

Rory took it with a relief that was physical pleasure. "Aye. I made a mistake of the first order in my reconnoitering of the Blois townhouse—I assumed Charles Blois and his daughter would both be at the exhibition at Somerset House. But she wasn't. She was home alone."

"And she surprised ye, and piked ye, and kept ye from taking any paintings?"

Leave it to Ewan so sum everything up so succinctly. "Aye."

"But did you see any more suspicious Vermeers?" Alasdair asked.

"No, but I did see that Hals portrait that Charles Blois mentioned to ye, Archie."

Archie uttered a crude word of satisfaction before he asked, "Did it interest ye as a collector, or as an independent expert?"

"The latter." Rory took a deep, necessary drink. Necessary to keep his mind focused on the conversation at hand, and not on the memory of Mignon Blois in her translucent nightie.

"Well?" Alasdair demanded, all aquiver, like a particularly eager gun dog on point. "What did you find out? Is it a forgery?"

"Can't tell without examining the painting in a great deal more detail, and in a great deal better light than I was able to do while housebreaking, and having a pike—or whatever the damn thing with an axe blade the size of Grosvenor Square is—pointed at me." He let himself collapse into a chair, and put his feet up on a hassock. Good God. It was only a little past midnight, and he was exhausted. This was what being piked did to a man. "Ye'll forgive me if my examination was incomplete."

Exhaustion was no excuse to Alasdair. "I'll forgive you if

you tell me what you're thinking in that devious mind of yours."

Rory took another restorative sip. "I'm thinking about Charles Blois."

"And if he's a forger?"

"If he is," Rory mused, "he's very, very good. Utterly superior. But I have my doubts that anyone could be that good." At Alasdair's skeptical scowl, Rory elaborated. "Let us look at him from another perspective. Blois has a priceless Verrocchio sculpture on loan to the Royal Society." He ticked his evidence off on his fingers. "He comes from a family with a well-known collection. He has a very fine house in Soho Square. Therefore he is not living in poverty—he doesn't need to forge Vermeers or Hals. Unless ye think the Verrocchio is a forgery, too."

"No." Ewan shook his head. "The statue has definitely been in the collection for years, and was last exhibited in Paris in seventeen and fifty-three."

"When Charles Blois was eight years old," Archie finished.

"Exactly. Very good, Archie. Ye *were* paying attention at school."

"Of course I was, ye manky git." Archie's reply was only a little hot. Because they all knew mischief, and not maths, had been his forte.

"So Blois is not forging sculpture," Ewan concluded.

"Just so." Rory went on. "And if he wanted money, all he had to do would be to sell that Verrocchio. The *on-dit* from Mr. Christie's is that the Duke of Bridgewater offered Blois ten thousand guineas for it."

Archie let out a long, low whistle.

"Just so," Rory agreed. "And if he has a Verrocchio that is worth ten thousand—and good God, what a price—why does he need to forge paintings?"

"Pride," Alasdair offered instantly. "Vanity. Accomplishment."

"And inquiries have revealed that he studied painting in his younger days," Archie added. "In the French system, he would have studied and copied all the great masters to learn his technique."

"Let's remember the English also learn the same way," Rory said. "Just to be fair. On any given day, Somerset House is full of copyists that no one could accuse of forging."

"That means they're just not good enough," Alasdair opined. "Yet."

Rory took another deep, fortifying drink of brandy before he decided to broach a new topic. "What do ye know about the daughter?"

"Miss Marie Chantal du Blois? Known as Mignon, twenty-two years old, considered something of a dark, Gallic beauty." Alasdair, per usual, was impeccably well-informed.

"Is that the lass?" Ewan asked. "The lass who piked him?"

"Seems so." Alasdair spoke with his usual confidence. "What about her?"

"Do ye think she's in it with him?" Rory asked. The question had plagued him since the moment she had so kindly decided to let him go. And before that, when she had spoken of hydrogen water and styptics. Before she piked him for no apparent reason, of course.

"'In it with him' in what?" Alasdair rose from his chair. "You said you thought Charles Blois was not forging paintings."

"Aye, that is what I said, isn't it?" Rory called his brain back under starter's orders. "I have no evidence to support the suspicion that Charles Blois is forging." He could feel their disappointment as if it were a physical thing. Because he, too, felt that keen sense of loss—if for an entirely different reason. "However," he continued. "I do think the matter bears further investigation."

"Charles Blois himself bears further investigation, or your young Mademoiselle Blois?" Alasdair had such a keenly perceptive light in his eye, that Rory felt as if he were the one being investigated.

"Neither. I think I'll leave the Blois family, *père et fille*, out of it, while I simply concentrate on the artwork."

"That would be the sensible, logical approach," Alasdair acknowledged. "But I'll wager all takers a guinea that our Rory can't possibly stick to such an outrageously simple plan."

Chapter 7

RORY KNEW THAT he was going to lose that guinea the moment he strolled into Somerset House, and saw Miss Marie Chantal du Blois standing there as fresh as a French daisy and as sweet as apple *tartine*.

And while he was thinking in such exaggerated, poetical comparisons, he decided that Mignon Blois was a dove in a henhouse in such a crowd—where most of the women present were fashionably overdressed, Miss Blois was dressed with exquisite simplicity in a white *chemise à la reine*, under an embroidered dove grey silk jacket that was perhaps a few years out of style, but which fit her delicate person exquisitely.

Though he did like her better in only her night clothes.

All in all, she was an exercise in restrained perfection. But her attire was nothing to the beauty of the woman herself. In the full disclosure of daylight she was a revelation—a gamine delight with skin the warm, blushing color of tea with cream, and hair and eyes of a black so dark, it reflected all light.

Yet, for all her dazzling, delicate beauty, she gave off that sense of restraint, of holding-back. There was a glint of something serious, even mysterious in the dark depths of her steely gaze that was disconcerting in such a soft-looking lass. Something innately French, that even all his years at school in Paris could not help him define.

Something that drew him to her—the hot flame desperate for the cool gray moth.

She was alone—or if not alone, her father was not visible—and seemed to be walking the galleries for her own pleasure. Except that she appeared too intent to be enjoying the outing—she did not smile, and though she looked at the masterpieces hanging on the walls with a well-schooled eye, her gaze would inevitably return to the Verrocchio statue displayed on a raised plinth in the center of the hall.

Or rather, now that he noticed, her gaze was following the people looking at the Verrocchio—studying them, almost as if she were gauging their reactions.

Curious. Delightfully, attractively curious.

So attractively curious, that wherever she went within the galleries, he went as well, following at a discreet distance, waiting and willing her to see him.

She disobliged him, and did not.

Rory toed his pride back into line, and drew nearer, learning everything he could glean from her presence. She was poised, with a fine balance between polite and guarded. She was graceful, with a lovely natural walk, elegant and economical, and not in the least bit mincing. He didn't like mincing—it smacked of artifice and concealment—so it was convenient that she didn't mince, because he had already decided to admire her.

And he wanted her to admire him. And failing that, he wanted her to at least *see* him.

So he decided to make his presence known, and stood close to her. Too close. Until she had no choice but to notice him.

"Oh, excuse me, please," she began. And then she looked up again, and recognition lit her eyes. As did dismay. "You!" she breathed.

"Me." He doffed his hat. "Good afternoon, Miss Blois. I almost didn't recognize ye with yer clothes on. How interesting that we keep meeting under the most artistic of circumstances."

"No," she countered in a fierce whisper. "We are not meeting. We are not acquainted. I do not associate with thieves."

"But we are already associating with each other, and are chatting in this charming, amicable manner, so I'm afraid there's no hope for it now. Which piece do ye like best? Oh, aye." He answered for her, before she could so much as close her gorgeous, astonished mouth. "The Diana. Excellent choice." He turned to survey the statue himself. "Exquisite. Priceless."

He could see the moment she took his teasing bait—her eyes widened in horror at the idea that he might have come to Somerset House to steal the priceless statue. "You wouldn't dare!"

It was a rather novel thing, being thought such a dangerous character. He liked it very much. It felt rather dashing. "Fear not. I'm abstaining this week. Clipped my wings, with yer pike, ye ken."

"It was a halberd." She corrected in that low whisper, resisting all his efforts at charm, and raising one acute eyebrow to give him a pert perusal. "But I can see that you are none the worse for wear. More's the pity."

And that was the moment that the President of the Royal Academy, Sir Joshua Reynolds—a man well known to Rory—noticed his reluctant companion. "Ah, my dear Miss Blois." He bowed to her and extended his hand. "How good of you to come to see the exhibition."

Rory decided that discretion was always the better part of valor, and discretely withdrew himself, so he might not be recognized. But not so far that he could not overhear their conversation.

"Oh, Sir Joshua." She curtsied very quickly and shook the man's hand, but she clearly had not wanted to be recognized by anyone, either. She stepped back from Sir Joshua, as if she might make a bolt for the door.

But there would be no hope for it—Rory placed himself squarely in her way.

"My dear Miss Blois." Sir Joshua turned to reveal another man who had accompanied him. "His Grace, the Duke of Bridgewater has expressed a wish to become acquainted with you."

"How kind." Miss Blois's cheeks flushed an unhelpfully becoming shade of pink, as she sank into a graceful curtsey. "Your Grace."

"Miss Blois." The duke bowed graciously over his food-stained waistcoat. "Are you enjoying this marvelous exhibition?"

"Yes, Your Grace. Quite so."

"Excellent. It seems more important than ever that such masterpieces be shown publicly in England, with such tragedies as we hear in the news coming daily from France."

Miss Blois ducked her head, all shy discretion at such a clumsy attempt at sympathy. "Yes. Such news has been most difficult to bear."

"Ah, but you are here, safely amongst us. And more importantly, your Verrocchio is here, safe and very sound, as well."

Miss Blois appeared not to be insulted by being judged less important than a sculpture—she managed a quick smile beneath her raised eyebrows. "Thank you, Your Grace."

"Call me Bridgewater, please," the older man was saying. "I must say, I was quite pleased to see you here. Your father, is he also pleased with the exhibition?"

"Yes. Yes, he is. Very much so." She glanced toward the door, as if once again contemplating escape, but Rory still stood between her and freedom, so she reluctantly chose the devil she didn't know, and returned to her conversation with the duke.

"You know, I've loaned a number of masterpieces as well. The Titian, of course"—the duke gestured vaguely to a large canvas depicting "Diana and Callisto" that took pride of place on the central wall—"as well as a Raphael, and my Rembrandt."

"Oh, yes." Miss Blois managed to look suitably impressed enough to make Bridgewater feel he had done all he needed to do.

"Well, then." He nodded at Sir Joshua and Miss Blois. "That's done then. I'll bid you good day." And away he went.

"Well, indeed." Miss Blois was clearly nonplussed.

"Well, my dear." Sir Joshua patted her hand. "I do believe you've made a conquest."

"Oh, gracious." Miss Blois put her hands to her pink cheeks. "I do hope not."

Rory decided it was relatively safe for him to re-enter the conversation. So long as he took control of it. "There is no hope for it, Miss Blois. Hello, Sir Joshua." He put out his hand, then turned to Miss Blois. "Sir Joshua and I are well acquainted, as I was once his humble student."

"Ah, yes." Sir Joshua smiled and took his hand. "I thought I saw a smashing pair of chestnut goers outside. Good to see you, as always, Mr.—"

"Ye did indeed see my magnificent pair," Rory broke in. But he was inordinately proud of his horses. Apart from art, they were his only major indulgence. "Miss Blois does not care for my team. She and I are old friends as well, ye see," he offered in explanation for his presence at her side. "We used to hunt together."

The lass made a strangled sound of outrage at what she no doubt thought was his infernal cheek, but Sir Joshua was oblivious to the unspoken conversation between them. "Ah, mademoiselle shoots, does she?"

"Oh, aye," Rory confirmed, with a deeply serious nod. "Amongst other weaponry."

Miss Blois tried manfully to turn the conversation. "Such a lovely exhibition the Royal Academy has put on, Sir Joshua. So many lovely paintings."

"Aye." Rory agreed. "So many pieces. And so valuable." He waggled an eyebrow at her. Provoking her was turning out to be rather fun—Mignon Blois's eyes grew even wider at his sheer audacity.

"Yes, but we have taken great security precautions," Sir Joshua assured them. "Tildesley Patent Alarm Locks, you know, on all the doors and windows. And Bow Street Runners hired as guards to watch the doors, as well."

"Oh, goodness." She seemed almost apologetic. "Such an expense."

"Oh, the Royal Academy has spared no expense for such treasures." Sir Joshua was clearly quite pleased with his precautions. "We must protect what is ours, even if it is only ours for a short while. I know that your family has had to endure a great deal in leaving your country, but we shall do everything possible to protect your magnificent collection."

"Thank you, Sir Joshua. You are everything kind. However…"

Sir Joshua had turned his eye to Rory. "I know you're interested in art, Mr.—"

"Yes, yes very much," Rory cut in before he could be identified as the Honorable Mr. Cathcart. "And in your security. This Tiddley, ye mention? I don't think I've heard of him," he lied.

"Tildesley locks," Sir Joshua clarified. "Patent alarmed locks used in many of the finer homes now. Let me show you."

Poor Miss Blois tried to prevent Rory from following the older gentleman by taking Rory's arm in the most wonderfully proprietary manner. "I am so sorry, Sir Joshua, but I have another appointment that requires me—"

"But I am very interested in Mr. Tildesley's invention," Rory broke in again. "Ye go on. I, myself, find the security of one's home and collections to be such an important matter."

Poor Miss Blois was utterly scandalized at Rory's apparent enthusiasm, and tugged at his elbow, as if she were trying to rein in a horse.

But Sir Joshua, who knew Rory's very real interest in the subject, proceeded with his information, oblivious to her discomfort. "Each of the doors and windows has its own alarmed lock that can only be turned off with its own key. And I'll tell you another secret, Miss Blois. We have adapted a Tildesley lock to sit under the statue. And in this instance, when the statue is lifted, and the weight removed from the spring lock, the bell within that lock will go off, and the runners will come running to seize the perpetrator."

"I say, that is clever."

Sir Joshua was pleased by the praise. "Quite ingenious, wouldn't you agree, Miss Blois?"

"Very much. Very, very clever. Bravo, Sir Joshua." Miss Blois was determined to turn the conversation yet again. "But we must not take up any more of your most valuable time. As I said, I have an appointment that I must rush off to—"

"Oh, too bad, Miss Blois." Rory disengaged his arm, and bowed to her before he turned back to Sir Joshua, knowing exactly how it would appear to her. "However, I should be delighted to stay and listen."

But deceptively dainty Mignon Blois was not so easily thwarted—she stiffened that secretly steely spine. "Oh, but you are promised at Lady Arbuthnot's as well. The dear lady cannot do without you. Thank you, dear sir." She curtseyed again to Sir Joshua. "But am afraid we both must go," she insisted, and took Rory's elbow in a grip that would have done a gunner proud. "*Au revoir*, Sir Joshua. Good day."

"Well," Rory commented as she whisked him out of the exhibition, "that was neatly accomplished. Well done, ye."

"You impossible man." She dropped his arm as soon as they were out in the courtyard. "Have you no shame? Have you no scruples at all?"

"The only ones I have, I'm sure I stole."

"Oh, *Bon Dieu*. You're utterly mad—quite irredeemable." She backed away a step or two before she tried to shoo him off like a stray dog. "Go away before I am obliged to call the watch."

He gave her one of his most charming smiles. "There is no watch in the daytime."

Frustration was written all over her very pretty face. But Miss Blois had reserves of character she had not yet tapped. "A pity." She crossed her arms over her chest in that delightfully uplifting manner that made his brain roll over on its belly, wanting to be scratched like the stray dog he in fact was. "Perhaps one of those runners inside would be vastly obliged to make your acquaintance? I understand that a good many runners are also thief takers."

"So they say." He'd used the Runners' services himself a time or two. But not today—today he had already done all he needed to do. "I concede the point to ye, Miss Blois."

"Well," she muttered under her breath as she strode off through Somerset House's stone portal. "It is a relief to find I am not the only one conceding."

"Never fear, my dear Miss Blois." He tipped his hat to her retreating back. "I am an old hand at all sorts of delicate concessions."

Chapter 8

MIGNON CAME DOWN the stairs in her best lavender watered silk evening *robe à l'anglaise,* and found her father admiring the huge floral bouquet that had been delivered a few hours earlier. "Are they not extravagantly beautiful?"

"The flowers? They are nothing to your beauty, my dear. But are they from an admirer?" Papa had a rather hopeful glint in his eye.

She was too flattered not to share at least a tiny bit of that hopefulness—no one in London had ever sent her flowers before. "According to the card, they are from a gentleman that I have just met—the Duke of Bridgewater."

"Bridgewater?" Her papa was open-mouthed with astonishment.

"Yes, I met him at the exhibition at Somerset House. Why?"

Papa was diverted by the mention of the exhibition. "Ah, you went. Very good. Did the Verrocchio not look stupendous in the center of the hall?"

"Yes, Papa, it certainly did, catching every eye, which is exactly what I am afraid of."

"Ah, *je m'en fiche!*" Papa waved off her concern. "You worry too much. But Bridgewater, he sent flowers like a young swain? Though he is rich, he is far too old for you.

He's fifty if he's a day."

"You know him?"

"But of course. He is one of the last great open-handed collectors of the day. It is he who tried to purchase the entirely of the Orléans collection, and in so doing convinced me to create the Blois collection. He has been, how shall I say, acquisitive about our collection's as-yet-unseen treasures."

"Oh, no, Papa. He did not mention that when we met." Mignon was suddenly feeling a great deal less flattered.

"No? But he could not know that he is the one who inspired me, or rather his fortune did. Yet, I find it strange he did not mention that he has a Pontormo, the *Portrait of a Halberdier*, from the Blois Collection."

That sinking feeling that always accompanied her father's casual talk of the Blois Collection was like a stone in her shoe, tripping her up and weighing her down. "Pontormo's *Portrait of a Halberdier*, or your Pontormo?"

"Mine, naturally. I would never part with an original Pontormo, had I one. But the original is gone—up in flames or scavenged for the gilding on the frame with the rest of my grandfather's collection when the mob took the chateau."

"So you sold a forgery to the most important collector in Britain?"

"Bah, I hate that word, forgery. The portrait was a magnificent work of art—it still is. Once the *duc* saw it, he had to have it. He couldn't praise it highly enough. I took the lease on this house with the proceeds of that sale. Did he not mention our dealings?"

"Not a word." The sinking feeling had her entirely submerged, holding her breath under the murky waters of her father's subterfuge. But she could see enough in those murky waters to realize that the Duke of Bridgewater was likely only after her to gain better access to her father's reputed collection of art. Or— "Oh, no, Papa. What if he suspects something? What if he found some irregularity in the Pontormo?"

"Calm yourself." Papa took her cold hand, and chafed it between his own. "You worry too much. There can be no irregularity. I know my Pontormo. I mixed the paints myself, by hand, from very old, very pure Italian pigments in the antique style. No, no, there is no irregularity. Depend upon it."

Her father could simply not conceive of his own vulnerability—of their vulnerability—or admit that he might have made a mistake.

"Oh, Papa." The very thought of Bridgewater's notice now made her feel so uneasy.

Papa was entirely unaffected by such qualms. "Will he be at the ball tonight?"

"The note on the flowers indicated so." Mignon sighed. All her enjoyment in the evening faded away. How she had much rather stay home now, and avoid it all.

Papa, however, was far more practical. "Then we had best go and meet him, and find out what is really on his mind."

She did not have long to find out—no sooner had their hired sedan chairs deposited them in front of a mansion on St. James's Square, than they were met by Sir Joshua Reynolds and the Duke of Bridgewater.

Papa was all bright eyes and shameless encouragement as Mignon made her curtseys. "Gentlemen, let me introduce you to my daughter, my angel Mignon, for she is my greatest treasure."

Sir Joshua demurred. "I had the honor of introducing your very beautiful daughter to His Grace only yesterday, Count Blois."

"Ahh. Very good. Now you must tell me"—Papa took Sir Joshua's elbow and began to steer him away—"how goes the exhibition, and what you plan for the summer show."

Which left Mignon with the large, slightly unkempt duke, who looked as creased as an unmade bed. "Mamselle." He nodded at her in lieu of a bow over his bulk. "Will you walk with me?"

"Yes, yes, go ahead, my child." Papa called his

permission over his shoulder.

There was no possibility of refusal. Mignon drew in a tight breath. "Thank you, Your Grace. I will."

"Very good, very good." The *duc* placed his hands behind his rather broad back, and began a slow, stately perambulation along the edges of the ballroom. "Norfolk has a very spacious room here," he observed, by and by. "What do you think it holds, ten, twelve couples? Of course my rooms at Bridgewater House, in Westminster, can hold twenty."

"How very spacious for dancing, Your Grace." Mignon said what she felt was required. "Of course your paintings— your wonderful collection—also needs room to breathe."

"Ah, just so!" He beamed at her. "How good you are to understand that. But your refined sensibilities are, no doubt, due to your being French. English gels are all twelve to a dozen, but you're like…a breath of fresh air."

"Yes, that is very nice of you to say, *Monsieur le Duc.* But my mother, you know, was as English as you are."

"Ah, was she? Better and better. No doubt she was a great beauty, too."

"You are very kind to say so. I remember her as such, but perhaps that is only a daughter's longing for her mother."

"Just so, just so."

They lapsed into silence—uncomfortable for her, though the *duc* showed some signs of unease as well. He was all pursed lips and puckered brow as they turned at the end of the room.

Though she dreaded to ask, she knew she must. "Pray forgive my impertinence, Your Grace, but I have a very great feeling that there is some topic that you are avoiding for politeness' sake."

The duke's grey, bushy eyebrows shot upward. "Oh, well, yes. Yes, you are quite remarkable. Of course you would be very acute. Very sensitive."

"Thank you." Mignon searched for the right words— encouraging but consolatory. "I should like to be sensitive enough that you should feel you could confide in me, Your Grace. For your own sake, if not for mine."

"Yes." He stopped, and nodded his head, as if he were gathering resolution. "Well, the truth is, it has to do with your father, and—" He stopped and looked around, as if he feared eavesdroppers.

Though her heart was clattering in her chest like a rickety tumbrel, she let him lead her toward the tall windows, where fewer people were to be had. "Yes? About my father?"

"And the Blois Collection."

"Oh, dear." The room began to narrow down to the spot on which she stood, as if she were in a tunnel. Every other sound faded until her ears were practically ringing with her own fear.

"Yes, well you see— Devil take me, but this is difficult to speak of."

She would not give in to the urge to run. She would not allow herself to succumb to the weakness in her legs, or the tight dread in her chest. She dragged in a shallow breath. "Yes, I understand. And I appreciate your discretion."

"I beg your pardon, Your Grace." A liveried footman stood behind the duke, bearing a silver tray with a card.

"Can't you see I'm busy?" the duke groused. But he still immediately took up the card, and read its contents. "Well, damn—oh, your pardon, mamselle. If you would be so good as to excuse me a moment?"

"Yes, of course." What else did one say to a *duc* who held one's future in his hands? Though her shivering heart could use the rest, the wait boded her quivering stomach no good.

Because there was worse to be had—no sooner had the *duc* departed, than the absolutely fearless Mr. Andrews sauntered over to her. "My dear Miss Blois," he said as if he had happened upon her purely by chance. "Good evening."

"Oh, no. You." She would have made her escape, but the duke had left her in a corner, in more ways than one.

"Me. Now that's not a very cordial greeting for an old friend." Mr. Andrews had no shame—he smiled easily, as if he attended such exclusive events every night. "I went to some considerable trouble to remove your inconvenient suitor for a few moments."

"Inconvenient? For whom?" The cheek of the man was absolutely astonishing. "Who let you in?"

"Lovely to see ye as well, Miss Blois." He took the hand she had not offered, and raised her glove to his lips. "Suffice it to say, I make friends wherever I go."

Oh, he was the most charming of gentleman rogues, there was no doubt about that. "There is, I suppose, no accounting for taste."

He was such a rogue that he laughed in agreement. "Quite. But there is something I must tell ye. Why don't we dance?"

"No." She instantly refused. God forbid she be in a thief's confidence—any more than she already was. "There is nothing I should like to hear from you, sir."

"It's important." He steered her a little deeper into the corner, and looked around in his furtive, thief's manner, as if he, like the *duc*, wanted to impart some great confidence. "Oh, damn his eyes, he's coming back. There's no time." Andrews backed toward the long glass doors at the end of the room. "Ye must meet me. Come to Brooks's," he suggested.

"A gentleman's club?" Mignon was even more astonished at his cheek than ever. "You are mad."

"Probably." He flashed that sparkling grin at her, and she felt all the irresistibility of his charm. "Brooks's!" he whispered once more before he slipped away into the crowd.

"Ah, my dear mamselle." Duke of Bridgewater had returned in all his pomp and glory. "Now, where were we?"

Mignon gathered what was left of her tattered her composure and threadbare courage to withstand the coming blow. "You were telling me about my father and his collection."

"Ah, yes." The duke himself took a deep fortifying breath. "I hate to have to tell you this, Miss Blois, but I arranged our meeting."

It was just as she feared. Dread seeped like cold sea water into her lungs, slowly drowning her. But still she had to ask, "Why, sir?"

"Because I must have it. I must. I am utterly possessed by it. It has permeated my spirit—it haunts me."

Mignon was all confusion—this was not at all what she had expected to hear. Perhaps the *duc* was being a gentleman, and trying to break the news to her gently? "What haunts you, Your Grace?"

"The Verrocchio Diana, of course."

"Oh." It took a long, nerveless moment for her brain to send the news to her lungs before she felt she could breathe again. Mignon took a gratefully deep breath—she did not know when she had been so relieved not to feel special.

"I am sorry for such an ungentlemanly behavior, but I am not myself," the duke admitted in apology. "I am a man obsessed. You must make him sell it to me. You must. I've offered him ten thousand guineas."

"You poor man." She shook her head, both in relief, and willing him to understand. "The Verrocchio is not for sale. It never shall be."

He frowned at her in complete consternation—like a fish out of water, wide-mouthed and gasping. Uncomprehending that anything he wanted might not immediately become his.

"I wish it were in my power to simply give her to you." Mignon was so relieved, she patted his hand in consolation. "You poor, darling man." And then she leaned up and placed an impulsive kiss upon his cool, ruddy cheek.

"Why, Miss Blois!" His Grace, *Monsieur le duc* was all astonishment—he put a hand to his cheek in disbelief. "You...kissed me."

She did not care if she had confounded him—so long as he did not want to put her papa in gaol, she would kiss him again and again. "I apologize, Your Grace. It was kindly meant. I did not mean it to be familiar, but as a consolation."

He looked as if she might well have smacked him as kissed him, so amazed was he. "I don't know when I've been—good God, but you're lovely."

"You are too kind, Your Grace." Mignon felt as if the weight of the world—her father's world full of forged painting—had just lifted off her narrow shoulders. "A kiss is small compensation for an artwork, but it is the best I have to offer."

"Is it now?" The poor man actually blushed pink with pleasure. "Aren't you just the most remarkable thing."

She was not remarkable. She was only herself. But she was happy. "Shall we dance?"

"Really?" His astonishment and his eyebrows climbed another notch. "Yes, yes, indeed."

But as she turned toward the dance floor with his stammering grace of Bridgewater, someone else caught her eye—a man who should not have even been admitted.

A man with entirely too much cheek. A man who was mad.

But the way he looked at her—in invitation to something other than a dance—almost made her feel remarkable. As if he were mad, not for her father's artwork, but for her, and her alone.

Chapter 9

MIGNON WAS STILL in that remarkable and hopeful mood the next morning, when she came down to find Papa at breakfast, taking his usual pains to mix his *café au lait* exactly to his liking.

"My darling, you are up early after a late night."

"It was you who had a late night, not I." After her dance with Bridgewater, Mignon had decided discretion was definitely the better part of valor, and taken a sedan chair home. Papa had stayed. She could only pray he had not gotten up to too much mischief. "Good morning, Papa." She kissed him on both cheeks.

"Good morning, my darling. But I thrive upon all this city hubbub, whilst you, my angel, prefer all that is quiet and calm."

"True," she acknowledged. "And speaking of all that is calm, I must tell you all about his grace, the Duke of Bridgewater."

"Yes?" Her papa was all eagerness to hear.

"The flowers were, as I suspected, a ruse to become acquainted with me, but it was all in the service of art, and his collection. He wanted nothing with the Pontormo—so you are all in the clear. He only wanted me to intercede to convince you to sell him the Verrocchio. Even though I told him it was not for sale."

"Ah. *Bon Dieu*. These Englishmen are all mad as hatters. It must be something they put in the tea."

"Yes, indeed." Mignon was too happy to object on behalf of her new countrymen. Besides, the duke did seem a little mad. As did others who would not be mentioned in her conversation with her Papa.

Perhaps madness was going around, like an influenza.

"*Pardon, Monsieur le Comte.*" Henri, stood in the doorway of the breakfast room. "There is a man to see you, sir, from the Society of Lloyd's Exchange in Cornhill Street."

"A man? Not a gentleman?" Papa looked to Mignon. "Henri is too nice about such things."

"He is a respectable man," Henri clarified, "a clerk of some kind, *Monsieur le Comte*. A senior clerk, I should think."

Papa shrugged. "No doubt a respectable, dull man, which will please you, my dear Mignon. Show him in to the salon, if you will, Henri."

Mignon followed her papa to meet the elfin man who appeared every small inch a senior clerk, and came up to introduce himself with a short bow. "Mr. Arthur Ossier, sir, from the Society of Lloyd's. My apologies for calling so early, sir," the clerk said. "But it was deemed imperative to collect your signature on the policy on the artwork by Verr—" The little man consulted his notes to read out the unfamiliar name. "Sig-nor Veer-oh-chee-oh."

"No, no." Papa smiled serenely. "I have taken no insurance on such a work—it is beyond price."

"Yes, exactly, sir. A special cover was taken by Sir Joshua Reynolds on behalf of the Royal Academy of Arts, that the artwork be insured against loss or damage in transportation and exhibition, as well as theft, by the Society of Lloyd's."

"Theft, you say?" Papa shot her a glance, perhaps thinking of their own recent encounter with theft, though she had not told him of her subsequent meetings with her gentleman thief.

The little man nodded ruefully. "There seem to have been rather more robberies of domiciles of late, sir."

Papa gave Mignon what she could only call a speaking glance—a glance that told her not to speak. "So we hear," he said noncommittally.

"Many of our wealthier citizens have taken to putting iron bars across their windows as a prevention against such thefts."

Papa shuddered dramatically. "God forbid. Like living in a gaol."

"As you say, sir." Mr. Ossier was all sad agreement. "But the artwork in question is not housed here, but in the exhibition space of Somerset House, which is where the cover is taken. If I may?" He opened a leather folio. "I shall need to obtain your signature upon the document."

"And the cost?" Papa was nothing if not frugal with his ill-gotten gains.

"At no expense to yourself, sir. All borne by Sir Joshua Reynolds of the Royal Academy, and His Grace the Duke of Bridgewater, patron." He spread the foolscap on the empty central table. "Once you sign, sir, the work of art is covered until it is returned to this house in good order."

"I just have to sign?"

"Yes, sir, and then it is insured against loss by flood, fire, accident, mischance, looting, sacking, pillaging, act of war, or theft."

"How delightfully thorough you English are."

At last Mr. Ossier smiled. "Thank you, sir."

Papa took up the pen Mignon hastened to bring him from the *escritoire*, dipped it into the inkwell she also held for him, and signed with his usual careless flourish.

Mr. Ossier was pleased—his elfin cheeks turned pink. "I thank you, sir." He sanded the signature, waved it dry and then carefully folded the policy, put it away in his case, and retrieved his hat from Henri. "By the by, sir." The clerk paused in the doorway. "Would you like to be present at the examination of authenticity?"

Papa stopped stock still in the middle of the Aubusson rug. "Examination of ...?"

"Authenticity, sir. Yes, Lloyd's now require it for

artwork, due to the current fluidity of the markets due to the bad business in France, if you'll pardon my saying."

"Of course." Papa waved away the entirety of the Revolution—he had more pressing problems.

"And, of course, you have just authorized the examination with your signature, so your most valuable work will be protected in such troubled times."

"Have I?" Poor papa's voice cracked, as if he had a cat in his throat.

"Yes, thank you." Mr. Ossier made another smart bow. "A mere formality. A specialist, the Honorable Mr. Cathcart, the Earl of Cathcart's youngest son, is an authority, I'm told. He is a Scotsman, but also a connoisseur, so they say, in the Old Masters, and has been engaged to conduct the examination Monday next."

Papa was too stunned to speak, and Mignon feared the two of them were gaping quite rudely at the poor clerk, who seemed to sense his visit was at an end. "Well, I've taken up enough of your time, sir. I'll see myself out."

Papa and Mignon said and did nothing until they heard Henri close the door behind the man. At which point Papa collapsed into a chair. "*Bon dieu.*"

Good God was only the beginning of the decidedly blue curse Mignon had been formulating. And even though she had warned her father of this exact sort of thing befalling him, she felt not even a smidgeon of satisfaction—only overwhelming worry. "This Mr. Cathcart, have you heard of him? Will he be able to tell?"

Papa passed his hand over his eyes, as if the thought pained him deeply. "He'll know. He discovered that hack Lefevre, but that was to be expected—*he* didn't even make his own paints, or use appropriate old canvas. And his technique! No *impasto*, no attempt at *sprezzatura*. Well..." Papa made a thoroughly Gallic sound of disapproval. "*Bon débarras*. Good riddance."

"But Lefevre was a painter," Mignon pointed out. "Could this Mr. Cathcart know sculpture so well?"

"Who knows?" Papa threw up his hands in despair. "But

my dear, at even the first faint huff of suspicion, the entire myth of the Blois Collection goes up in smoke. Every thing I've sold, every single piece, will be examined to the last speck of ultramarine and vermillion, and we'll be ruined. Ah." He closed his eyes as if he might block out his vision of a bleak future. "We live in a crass, grubbing world with no *finesse* or *élan*. No faith or trust."

Mignon refrained from pointing the ironies of such a statement, while Papa poured himself a medicinally large helping of cognac. But they could not just drink and despair—they had to do something.

She firmed her resolve as much for him as for herself. "Then we will simply keep this man, Mr. Cathcart, from examining the Verrocchio." But how? "You could recall the Diana from the exhibition—we'll go directly to Sir Joshua, and tell him you have changed your mind about loaning the statue."

"No, no." Papa waved her suggestion off. "I cannot do that. The effect would be the same—all suspicion. I have just put my head under their guillotine, and loosened my collar to make it all the more convenient." He lapsed back into his chair with his head in his hands for a moment before he sprang back up, reaching for her. "I must keep you out of this. You must leave London." He gripped her hands as if he would shake his urgency into her. "You must take the money from the sale of the Vermeer, and go to America. You are young and beautiful, and they are friends of the French."

"Oh no, Papa." As if she would leave him to face the wolves alone.

"You must. It will be easier for me to bear, if I know you will not be touched."

"Papa." She tried to speak calmly—far more calmly than she actually felt. "I'm not going to leave you in your hour of need. No, we *du Blois* stick together."

In the hallway outside the salon, Mignon could hear the rapid advancement of feet, before Henri slipped through the door. "*Monsieur le Comte*, there is another man, a gentleman,

Lord Carrington, come to call. About a painting by Hals, he says."

"Papa!"

Papa glanced up at the painting in question, and managed to look both pained and guilty. "Such an erudite young man."

"The Hals?" Mignon dropped her voice to a whisper. "But Papa, you only just finished—how does he even know?" And this new lord was not the first person to show interest in the Hals—her gentleman thief had been just as particular.

Her papa could only give her one of his deprecating shrugs. "I might have said something. He introduced himself at Mr. Christie's auction of my Vermeer, when it fetched such a staggering sum, and I might have let slip that I was also in possession of the Hals."

"Oh, Papa." So by now all of London—both the criminal and aristocratic halves—knew of the painting. And the paint could not even possibly be dry. "You must send him away."

"Yes, yes, I must." Papa sighed with resignation. "Send him away, Henri. Send him away, though it pains me. Quickly, man"—he waved his hands at Henri—"before I change my mind."

"Papa, you must realize this *charade* is finished." Mignon didn't care if she had to beg. "Please!"

"Why? Why not? Why should I not have my triumph over them all—over all of them, aristos and peasants alike. They stole everything we had, and if I have stolen it back, piece by piece, then I am not ashamed. Let them come. I will tell them all. I will shame them and their experts and their connoisseurs alike. I will triumph, I tell you." But his voice gave away to despair.

"Papa." She wrapped her arms about him. "We will find a way. We will triumph." But they had to start by taking the Verrocchio back before it could be examined. If only she could sneak into Somerset House as effortlessly as her gentleman thief had snuck into their home—

The idea came to her just like the proverbial thief in the night. All of a sudden, it was there—and idea so outrageous, so daring, she felt a little bit mad.

Mignon raised her eyes to see the Hals portrait looking down at her with an encouraging twinkle in his eye. Encouraging her to be outrageous. Encouraging her to dare. "Papa? Where is Brooks's Club?"

"St. James's." Papa's tone was flat and disinterested with despair. "Next door to number sixty. It doesn't have its own number. So eccentric, so English, that."

"Yes, very English, Papa. Madly so." She kissed his cheek. "I think I'll go and join them in a fine piece of madness." She stood and straightened her skirts. "You leave it all to me."

Chapter 10

RORY CATHCART WAS just turning up St. James Street toward Brooks's from his cramped office at Mr. Christie's Auction rooms on Pall Mall—employment was playing havoc with his self-importance—when he saw the improbable sight of the delightfully determined Miss Mignon Blois approach the steps of the impenetrable gentleman's club, and try to catch the inscrutable doorman's eye.

Today she was attempting to go about *incognito*, wearing a wide, black *bergère* hat draped with a fine black lace veil, over a dove grey silk *robe à l'anglaise*, dripping with more black lace at collar and cuffs. The effect was quite of the mode, and understatedly fashionable, as he had come to expect of her, but undeniably French.

Rory put his hand to his hat, and started up the street at a run.

"Mr. Andrews?" he could imagine the burly chap guarding the door—a former prizefighter—saying to her. "Don't know any damn Andr—"

"Why, *Mademoiselle*." Rory tipped his hat to her as if he had only just that moment doffed it. "Do come away from there." He escorted her away before the doorman could get a good look at her fair face. Or call him Mr. Cathcart. "Ye'll give Rudyard an apoplexy, asking to be admitted like that."

"But I was not asking—" Beneath the veil, her fair face suffused with some combination of indignation and embarrassment. Whichever it was, the effect was utterly charming. "Oh, I see you take delight in acting the rogue."

"I do, indeed," he admitted without a shred of remorse. "What on earth are ye doing haunting St. James's?"

"Looking for you, of course. Why else would I come to Brooks's Club? You said to meet you here."

"I did indeed. But my dear Miss Blois, ye were meant to send a note first."

"You did not say that." She was all exasperation—her lovely brow puckered in a frown. "You said—"

"Aye, and that was very imprecise of me." He took her arm and steered her down the pavement toward the slopes of Green Park. "But I'm an art thief, not a secretary. Ye'll have to give me some leeway."

Much to his surprise, Miss Blois did not even attempt to lecture him. Instead she nodded, all eager conviction. "Yes, I am very glad to hear that, as it is in that capacity that I have come to speak to you on a matter of urgent business."

He was instantly leery—this was the lass who had spoken of hydrogen water. "What kind of business?"

"Urgent business," she repeated. "In your line of business." She leaned closer and spoke in a low voice, lest any of the passersby notice. "I find I have need of someone with your talents and skills."

Better and better. He had many talents, and still more skills, the thought of which ought to make him blush. But they did not—they were too useful. And far too pleasurable. "In what particular capacity, Miss Blois?"

"I need you to gig a case."

"What?" It took him a moment to translate the vulgar, cant term. "Oh, ye mean to break into someplace—to burgle." She could not have shocked him any more if she had said she *was* the one forging paintings. "Mademoiselle Blois, wherever did ye learn such language?"

"I was not born yesterday, Mr. Andrews. I have met my

share of scoundrels." Her pointed gaze told him she counted him in that number.

"I see. I must rearrange my impression of ye."

"By all means, do. Because what I have in mind is a bit more—" She lowered her voice to a whisper, and leaned even closer to impart her secret. "*More* than a mere burglary."

Rory could not imagine sweet Miss Blois engaging in anything so dishonest—so bloody cheeky—as a burglary. And he had imagined her doing many and various things— most of which involved night clothes.

But far be it for him to discourage her. "How much *more?*" He gave her his best confidential, tell-me-all-your-secrets smile. "Whom do ye want to burgle?"

"Not a who, a what—Somerset House."

Rory nearly tripped on the uneven grass. "Ye're mad. Not on yer life. Or mine, for that matter."

She grasped his forearm. "But what if I told you it *was* on my life?"

He took a step back so he might take a good hard look at her. A look that might make him see past her beauty and fragile air, and examine the very real possibility that perhaps Miss Mignon Blois was more of a scoundrel than even he might have thought.

"Ye are mad. Why on earth would ye want to break into Somerset…" It came to him with horrible, sudden clarity. "The Verrocchio."

She nodded grimly. "The Verrocchio."

"But it belongs to ye!"

"Well, it is not exactly mine—it is 'in the family,' if you will. But that has nothing to do with it."

"It has everything to do with it," he insisted. "Why do ye want to steal a statue ye already own?" He wanted to shake her—just a little. "Why? Is it for the notoriety?" he prompted. Stranger things had been done to increase the visibility, and therefore the value, of an art collection. "The money?"

"No, not at all." Her reply was emphatic. "Quite the

opposite. The less attention paid, the better. And there is no money to be made. The Verrocchio is not for sale."

"But stealing it—if such a thing were possible, and I'm not saying it is—would garner an *enormous* amount of attention." He could imagine the banner headlines Archie would write for the Spectator now.

"If it is money you are concerned about, I will pay you for the job," she pressed. "Not as much as the value of the statue, of course—it's worth at least ten thousand pounds."

"Aye, and there have got to be at least a thousand Bow Street Runners surrounding it." He started walking again. "I don't like the rate of exchange."

"You exaggerate. There are not so many as that."

"There are more than I could ever deal with. And there are more than Runners to deal with—the whole place has been alarmed to the teeth. Weren't ye listening to Sir Joshua the other day?"

"Yes, but surely there is something…"

"Nay."

She stilled, and the animation drained from her face, like a flower wilting from lack of sun. "Does that mean you won't do it?"

"Nay," he repeated, only gentler this time. "I won't. I can't." For many reasons involving ethics and his reputation, and the fact that he was not, in reality, a particularly good thief. He was no longer the thief he had been in his boyhood at all.

"Are you *sure*?" Her voice was soft and pleasing and very, very hard to resist.

He tried a little bit harder. "Quite sure. I'm sorry. But I thank ye for thinking of me. I'm flattered."

She was everything dejected. "I do not want to flatter you, I want to hire you." She heaved a big sigh out of her delicate little dove grey chest. "Then could you give me another name, as a professional reference?"

"Another thief? Good God. Are ye quite serious?" There was no way on earth that he would, or could, give her over to a real, actual thief—the Blois townhouse would be picked clean in days.

"Yes. I told you, I must get it."

He had to dissuade her. "Ye've seen the way the Verrocchio is protected. The locks and bolts, and all the runners, not to mention all the various and sundry members of the Royal Academy, and members of the public who fill the galleries."

"Well"—she turned those enormously appealing black eyes up to his—"I was hoping to leave those sort of details to your experience."

He felt as if he were drowning in her plea. "Ah. Aye, my experience. Well, experience will only get ye so far, and I'm afraid it won't be far enough. Those are not mere details."

"But I must— I must do something. Surely there is another—"

There could be no others.

"I'll tell ye what," he said before his brain could catch up with his mouth. "I'll sleep on the idea. It's too late to go there now—the galleries at Somerset House will be closed. But we'll go round there together in the morning, and have a look, shall we? We'll tout the case"—he gave her the thieves' cant—"tomorrow."

"Really?" Her smile was a warm sunrise after the darkest of nights, dawning softly across her face. "Oh, excellent." She turned and put out her hand for him to shake, like a gentleman. Just as if they were two men, on any pavement, anywhere in the city, sealing a well-made bargain.

But she was not a man. She was everything small and soft and feminine and enticing. Everything he wanted. And would do anything to get. Even break into Somerset House.

And he had taken her hand before he had time to think. Before he had time to warn himself, or prepare for the delicious shock of her cool, delicate flesh meeting his.

She gripped his hand evenly, with firm, unyielding restraint, and he felt an entirely different part of himself— something deep within his chest—stir to life. Something entirely different from casual infatuation or shallow lust. Something warm and earnest and protective.

Oh, dear God. He was an idiot—she had, with one flutter of her lashes, made him so.

Well, in for a penny, in for ten thousand pounds. "Why don't ye let me see ye home, Miss Blois. Or as the day is young, let me show ye a bit of London."

"No, thank you, Mr. Andrews. I know London quite well enough. My mother was English, you know."

He didn't know, though he should have. He'd have to make a note to be more careful in his research and reconnaissance next time. "Then why don't ye show London to me? I'm only lately come up to town from Scotland, ye see."

"Scotland?" The light in her face waned into skepticism—she put up her guard. "I had rather keep our dealings on a more professional footing, if you don't mind."

He did mind, but a fellow had to try. "Certainly we can keep our acquaintance professional. It is professional to understand intimately all the needs a client might have."

She still looked skeptical, her natural reticence and personal modesty making her regard him out of the corner of her eyes. "Had we not better meet in the morning?"

He gave in to the surprising strength of her restraint. "Yes, that would be lovely. But I find that such jobs are most successful when all the parties involved are entirely relaxed and at ease, so why don't ye come to my house for a nice leisurely breakfast, and—"

"Mr. Andrews." Her objection shimmered across her breathless voice. "I most certainly will not. We will keep any and all association between us strictly governed."

Again, a fellow had to try. "Quite right, Miss Blois. Forgive me. I'll meet ye at the corner of Coventry and Haymarket tomorrow morning, at ten o'clock sharp."

And out came the sun—her smile spread across her face in pleased relief. "Ten o'clock it is."

She nodded twice before she replaced her veil and swept away down the lawn, and out of sight in the trees.

And Rory went home to pour himself a drink. A large drink. Large enough to take a hot bath in.

Chapter 11

THE DANGEROUS, AND dangerously charming Mr. Andrews bowled up to the corner of the Haymarket and Coventry streets in that high perch phaeton so tall and dazzling and frightening, it took her breath away. And from the moment he handed her up, she could not seem to catch her breath for the entirely of their journey down the Haymarket and onto Cockspur Street, until they swung onto the Strand, where traffic made a breakneck pace impossible.

"That's the King's Mews." Mr. Andrews pointed with his whip as they looped around Charing Cross. "With the all the King's men."

"Yes?" She craned her neck back to see what he was talking about, but no group of horse followed. "Do you refer to the groomsmen?"

"They're not just grooms," he informed her. "They are ex-military men, mostly veterans of the North American wars—the king having a soft spot for his soldiers. And they are also more than mere soldiers—they are very often former cavalry troopers, and hard men."

"I did not know that. But what does that have to do with us?"

He did not answer directly, but continued his nonsensical travelogue, pointing to a mansion on the south side of the street. "And that is the Duke of Northumberland's House."

"So? He is nothing to do with us." Although she was quite sure His Grace the *duc* did have one of her father's forgeries—a tiny, luminous *faux* Rembrandt—hanging in his famous picture gallery.

"My information tells me the duke keeps a large host of well-trained footmen, who resemble nothing such much as a private army, and has done so since Wilkes' election riots some twenty-five odd years ago."

Before she could ask what point such information was meant to make, he reined his pair to a stop before the tripartite arch of their destination. "And here is Somerset House, with all its bustle and guards laid on for the course of the exhibition. And do ye know what's right up there past Catherine Street?"

"The Drury Lane Theatre?"

He shook his head as if she were the veriest infant. "Bow Street and the magistrate's office. Where the runners come from. And ye want to stage a robbery for a ten-thousand pound piece of artwork in the middle of all this." He made a neat circle before her. "Very handy. I can practically taste the bread and water."

Mignon didn't dare accuse him of losing his nerve—not when she was rapidly losing her own. It was one thing to think about breaking the law, and breaking into a hallowed institution, but it was quite another to ask another person to risk everything they had to do so.

So she saved her breath to cool her porridge, as these English liked to say, and silently followed him into the crowded exhibition rooms as he walked and looked and studied the layout.

At least that was what she assumed he was doing—she was just getting nervous. Inside her gloves, her palms had gone damp with apprehension.

And they were only "touting the case," as he had said.

But besides looking, it seemed as if her thief might be succumbing to the Diana's charms. Time and time again he circled back to the middle of the hall, staring at the

Verrocchio. And then at Mignon.

"What is it?" she finally asked.

"I could swear." He very gently took her face in his hands, and tipped her chin to one side, narrowing his eyes in contemplation. "Aye. I see it. There is a remarkable resemblance."

She twisted her chin out of his supple, thieving fingers. "Do not be ridiculous. I am not three hundred years old."

"Most decidedly not." He gave her one of his slow roguish smiles. "But just to be clear, where were ye in the middle part of the fifteenth century?"

Mignon kept her porridge cool, and let Mr. Andrews lead her on another seemingly casual ramble about the hall, before they fetched up in front of an empty mantelpiece. Mr. Andrews busied himself for a moment with an examination of the medieval tapestry on display as a fire screen in front of it, but then seemed only to be consulting his own image in the mirror hanging above.

Mignon was about to give him her less-than-flattering opinion of such a self-centered waste of her time, when she saw that he was in actuality tracking the movements of a footman—actually one of the liveried Bow Street Runners—who seemed to be tucking something into a small broom closet under the wide marble stair.

"Wait here," Mr. Andrews directed. "And make a bit of an ass of yer lovely self, if ye can manage it."

Mignon had no time to voice her outrage at his execrable language, before he slipped away behind the velvet ropes that had been set up to cordon off the area behind the stair to visitors. Belatedly realizing he meant to investigate the closet, she quickly stepped in front of the footman on guard, and tried to create a diversion by fumbling and dropping her hat pin so that the man was obliged retrieve it for her.

Her play acting must have worked, because before she could re-secure the black felt *bergère*, Mr. Andrews reappeared at her side just as suddenly as he had disappeared. "Nicely done, Mignon."

And before she could protest his over-familiar use of her family name, he signaled her to silence, took her arm, and steered her in the wake of a one of the liveried footmen-guards switching places with another.

Mr. Andrews surreptitiously checked his pocket watch before launching into a lengthy exposition on a small portrait. "Oh, aye, lass, do examine closely this Rembrandt. Old Master. Take note of the salient feature of the contrast of the beautifully revealed subject emerging from the dark background…" His lecture trailed off as the guard they were following disappeared behind a door.

"Wait here," Mr. Andrews instructed again.

"And make an ass of myself?"

His slow smile of appreciation was devastating in its charm—she instantly felt warm all over, as if she was bathed in a soothing cup of tea. "No. Once was more than enough to ask of ye. Just enjoy yerself for a few moments, while I look into things."

Mignon hid her pinked cheeks in contemplation of Rembrandt's dramatic juxtaposition of light and dark—*chiaroscuro,* she could have told Mr. Andrews, or anyone else who asked. But no one did, because Mr. Andrews returned before she had even got to an examination of the masterful brushwork.

"Well, that was instructional."

Instruction could be good or bad. "How?"

He did not answer. "Come walk with me."

He took her out into the fresh spring wind roaring up off the Thames for what became a long, leisurely, but silent stroll about the courtyard, before he led her just as silently out onto the Strand, where he waved away his tiger—a shifty-looking young fellow who lounged about ogling passing females instead of tending to the horses' heads.

But if Mr. Andrews did not care what his tiger did, then it was no business of hers.

But about that which *was* her business—the recovery of her father's Verrocchio—she most certainly would ask. "Are you going to tell me what you found instructional behind that door?"

"I found a guard's room, where they take their ease whilst off duty." He turned her to walk eastward along the Strand. "And some information about the charwomen who come in the night to tend to the place."

"What on earth do charwomen have to do with us?"

He shook his head and smiled, all at the same time. The effect made a hot *pot de crème* of her brain. "Ye'd be surprised."

"How so?" she managed.

"Before I tell ye, I feel it is my duty to first try dissuade ye from this particular endeavor." He linked his arm with hers. "I know a charming little gallery on Pall Mall we could very easily knock off, just to get our feet wet before we move directly into full-fledged catastrophe."

"No." While she appreciated his cheerful candor, she had to convince him that only the retrieval of the Verrocchio would do. "There is no time for any other."

"Then at least tell me why we must steal this particular statue—why steal something that already belongs to ye?"

"Well, you do not think I would steal something that does *not* belong to me, do you? That would be…dishonest." She had certain scruples that had to be maintained, even in the midst of thievery.

"Ye don't say." He scrubbed his hand through his hair, disrupting the smooth sandy queue. "Look here. The Diana statue will be returned to ye when the exhibition is over— why not wait until it's back in yer home, and steal it then, without a bit of bother? That's the sort of easy caper for which I would be delighted to offer my services."

She had to make him understand. "If I could do that then I would not need your services, would I? You do not understand. This is not a jape or a prank or a whim. I must get that statue away from here or else…There is no 'or else.' I simply must, and for that I need real, professional, criminal help. And you are the only criminal I know."

"I see." He did not, really—she could tell by the frown etched between his brows. But he was trying. "I must look at the facts impartially. We cannot get in or out through the alarmed doors. We cannot get in or out through the alarmed windows. We can't get rid of the runners. We simply—"

"Cannot get in or out."

He turned to regard her with those bright blue eyes. "I didn't say that."

There was something about him—a calm sort of mischief—that lit the dry kindling of hope within her chest. "Then you have an idea?"

He winched up one eye, as if he was not yet prepared to say. "A faint inkling of an idea. Walk with me." He let out a sharp whistle that brought the tiger leading the pair in their wake.

Mignon tried to bank the warming light of her enthusiasm, and allowed him to lead her along.

"I think better on my feet," he explained. "So, no in and out…." He muttered half to himself, and sidestepped just in time to avoid being splattered by the contents of a pail emptied from the alley, where two tired old scullery maids were sitting down in the thin sunshine to smoke their pipes in all their worn, soggy-skirted glory. "Like birds," he murmured, "drying their wings in the sun."

"'Birds of a feather flock together' you English say," Mignon remarked. "Or as the French would have it, *'Qui se resemble s'assemble.'*"

Her gentleman thief frowned, as if he could not quite ponder out what she was saying. "Those who resemble each other, assemble together?" And then, his face cleared and his eyes went wide and bright with the spark of an idea. "Oh, God, yes."

He grabbed her by the shoulders, and before she understood what he meant to do, he graced her with a wildly enthusiastic, smacking kiss.

Her breath froze in her throat, only to be thawed by the warm tingling that emanated from her lips. Mignon did not remember when she had been so shocked—excepting that moment when she had finest encountered her gentleman thief—until he spoke, and shocked her anew.

"Devil take me, Miss Blois. I think ye've got it!"

Chapter 12

"QUICKLY NOW, MISS Blois." Rory whistled sharply for Archie to bring up the phaeton. Now that he had made up his mind, there was no time to waste. "Let me hand ye up."

"Sir, if you think I will allow you any further liberties, just because I let you kiss me—"

"My dear Miss Blois, that kiss was not a liberty. That kiss was a celebration of ye solving the mystery of how we are going to steal yer statue."

Mignon Blois went still with excitement. "Then you *are* going to steal it?"

"*We* are. But only if ye get in. Quickly now."

She cast a wary eye upon his wickedly fast little carriage. "Where are we going?"

"Petticoat Lane, away to the east"—he pointed the way up the Strand—"to test yer resolve. I cannot do this thing without ye, so I want ye to take a long last look at the blue sky, the green grass, the blowing trees, and the gray river, all of which I loathe, personally, which means I won't much mind a nice long stint in a small dank prison. But ye may mind. Ye may like yer liberty."

"My liberty? My help? You are mad." Her look of consternation—all lush lips crushed between white teeth—was more than enough to convince him he would be mad *not* to include her. "You do not need me to put my hand to this dough. I am not a thief."

He could not help the smile that slid across his face at her mangling the French idiom for aiding and abetting into English. "Nonetheless, ye'll do, Miss Blois. Ye'll do quite nicely. But ye'll have to agree right now to two particular things."

It was something of a revelation to watch her decide—to watch her quiet wariness slowly gave way to the temptation. He smiled encouragingly—raising his brows and nodding—to help her along the crooked path.

"What sort of things?" she finally asked.

He was not going to make it so easy. "Ye have to agree before I tell ye."

He could almost see the change—those dark eyes took on a steely glint of purpose, and she took a deep breath to calm her growing excitement. "And if I agree to help you, then will you agree to steal the Diana?"

He took his own deep, calming breath. "Aye, I'll help ye steal the Diana." God help him, but he would likely do anything she asked, even if she didn't agree to help him.

He was rewarded when her face was instantly suffused with a vermilion pink sunrise of pleasure. "Then I agree as well." Her voice was all breathless delight. "I am quite determined to go to any lengths to retrieve the Verrocchio."

Oh, he knew in that moment that he would never want to knowingly disappoint that hopeful, trusting, happy, heart-shaped face. He would do anything—even the impossible, because how would she look at him then, when he had got her Verrocchio for her? How would she reward him?

It made the prospect of ruining his career quite worth it.

Of course, infatuation was no basis for making a sound decision. He firmed his voice, to make it sound more businesslike. "Good. That's settled. Now, the first thing is that ye have agreed to follow my lead unconditionally." When she nodded he went on. "And the second is that ye'll have to get in the carriage."

Despite just having promised to help him, and do as he

bade, she eyed the yellow monstrosity as if it were a spider.

"It's too late to turn back," he reminded her. "Ye've already agreed, and I mean to take ye at yer word."

Poor Mignon Blois gathered her courage along with her skirts, and climbed up, and set her hands to the edge of the seat in a death grip. Which he very kindly noticed. "I shall go it at a crawl, Miss Blois. I shall be everything prudent and sedate, and let ye breathe."

He was true to his word, and took it at a nun's pace straight up Strand to Fleet Street, and on through the Temple Bar toward East London, through the working, bustling, swearing, sweating, shouting heart of the city. The West End and all its refinements had much to recommend it, but it was the east of the city that Rory loved best— where the men and the city worked as almost one animal. It was the part of the city that reminded him best of the wharves of Leith, at the watery edge of Edinburgh, where he had spent his formative years as an unacknowledged by-blow of the Earl of Cathcart. And where, despite the intervening years of education and erudition, he still felt most at home.

What delicate Mignon Blois and her Parisian sensibilities might think of East London, he could not say. Nor did she. But she did loosen her grip on the seat rail enough to take a level-eyed look around her. She was so sweet and serious and earnest and determined, that he almost hated to corrupt her by taking her into the maelstrom that was the used clothing market of Petticoat Lane.

But he took her there anyway.

The street itself was no more than the narrowest of lanes, made even narrower by the crowding of awnings hung thick with used clothing of all sorts and descriptions, the smell of which was as pungent as the colors were faded. So narrow and crowded was the street that Rory made no attempt to risk the bright polish of his phaeton, and abandoned his equipage to his tiger's— Archie in raffish disguise—dubious care.

As there was nothing he could really do to prepare her,

he simply took her hand and waded into the sea of humanity like a seasoned mariner.

With Mignon holding fast and bobbing along in his wake, Rory made straight for Ruby's, a tiny little hole-in-the-wall of a shop in the most tumble-down of buildings. But Ruby's prices were the best, and her discretion was assured—once he passed her a few extra bob.

Within two minutes of passing under the creaky portal, he had a suitable ensemble collected. "Here." He thrust the messy pile of messier clothing—a rough, patched, quilted petticoat, over a gray, moth eaten shawl, and a dingy once-white cap—at a wide-eyed Mignon Blois. "These, I think will do well for ye."

"These?" She turned over the well-worn cap. "But I will look an utter dowd."

He gave her his most conspiratorial and charming—and damned if he didn't know it—smile. "If ye'll insist upon frequenting criminal circles, my dear, ye can't be choosy."

He gave himself the pleasure of turning her by the delicate architecture of her shoulders, and pointing her in the direction of a vaguely curtained dressing area. "Go ahead and take off yer clothes."

"Mr. Andrews." A hot blush of madder rose painted her soft cheeks. "I know I said I was prepared to go to any lengths, but I fear you have mistaken me—"

Such a charming combination of innocence and insistence. "Ye're quite safe from me, Miss Blois. It is only, as they say in the theatre, dress rehearsal time. Ye'll go in there with yer pile"—he pointed at the curtained area—"whilst I shall repair over there"—he tipped his chin toward a nearby tower of clothing—"to await yer transformation." Like a gorgeously-colored butterfly forced back into a cocoon.

"Well, if it is a necessary part of the plan." She eyed the curtain with clear skepticism.

"It is indeed. Ruby the Rag Woman will guard yer modesty, as will this heap of clothes that will make it impossible for me to see ye. I promise, Miss Blois, not to peek, if ye will promise the same."

Her attempt not to smile brought dimples into the warm roses on her cheeks, and he wondered anew how on earth he was going to keep himself from disappointing her.

By being clever, and observant, just as he always was—that was the key.

At the moment, the key to his survival was not looking as the delicate and delectable Miss Blois un-pinned her hat. Not noticing the soft swirl of a curl at her nape, before she disappeared behind the rag-thin linen curtain to begin slowly disrobing.

To contradict the strange lethargy that seemed to settle into his bones at the thought of her soft, warm skin, or the memory of her in the thin lawn of her nightdress, Rory paced as far away as the small confines of the shop would allow. Which was approximately three feet and back.

Accordingly, the rest of his time was spent with his eyes closed, listening to the soft shushing sound of fabric sliding and settling behind the curtain. "How are ye progressing, Miss Blois? I realize it might be difficult without a maid."

"I am not so fine that I cannot dress myself, Mr. Andrews. Though I am not sure I want to put this mouse-dropping of a cap on my head before I have washed it in lye soap."

"Ruby gives all the clothing a good dunking before she puts it out, don't ye Ruby?" he appealed to the shop's owner. "Ye'll not get any lice in this shop. I wouldn't have brought ye here otherwise. Now come, let me see ye," he demanded.

Mignon pushed back the curtain to reveal her looking not unlike a fairy masquerading as a human—she was too delicate and pretty to really make an entirely convincing charwoman. But still, the clothes did make her look every inch the dowd.

"Oh, that's nice." He admired the worn edges of her apron. "Aye, that's just awful." He could not resist the urge to rumple her dark silky hair, before he tucked it into the mouse dropping of a hat—such an apt turn of phrase.

"Ye're perfect."

"Perfectly awful," she groused over her blush.

"I'd say ye're awfully perfect. The cap hides yer beauty nicely. Turn round for me, would ye?"

She made a slow, but perfect pirouette, looking over her shoulder at him the whole time.

Rory could feel the battlements around his heart start to crumble, look by solemn, blushing look. "Aye," he confirmed when he had found his voice in the rubble. "Ye'll make an admirable charwoman."

"Ah!" Her dark eyes gleamed with appreciative understanding. "So I am the charwoman. And what about you?"

"Picture a black coat with red and white woven trim, with a white-powdered bag wig."

Her eyes widened as slow recognition dawned. "Oh! You are to steal one of the runners' coats!"

He winked at her in reward. "I am. What do ye think?" He pantomimed playing a stiff-postured guard leaning against the wall—turnabout was fair play, and he didn't mind if he gave her a good look at himself. "Shall I look like a heartless thief taker?"

"With the right trimming, and proper shoes and stockings instead of boots, you will be perfect."

"I will indeed. Because there is a closet under the stairs at Somerset House, full of such costumes. And I hope in the heat of the moment, they will not miss one coat, more or less."

"In the heat of what moment?"

"We'll get to that later. Now, back to ye. Do ye know how to scrub a floor? I realize that ye're the daughter of an aristocratic *comte*, but what we'll need ye to do is find yer hard-working birds of a feather, and flock together, if ye see what I mean?"

"The charwomen?"

"Exactly. I've had to guess at their mode of dress, but as they come in at night, I'm guessing their clothing will be less regular than say, maids who work for private households.

But no matter what, scrub just like them, because just after midnight, I shall expect all hell to break loose inside that museum, and ye, my dear charwoman, will need to hang on to yer bucket."

She was smiling at him. "A charwoman. Well, this has to be a first." A happy, delighted smile that spread mischief across her face like raspberry jam.

Jam he would lick off in—

"I see it now—I can see your plan. Mr. Andrews, it is quite genius." Her praise brought him back to the present.

It wasn't genius, just a long-shot of a silly goose of a plan. A plan that may yet get the two of them a long cool spell in a cold dank gaol. Or perhaps not.

Perhaps he could explain his way out of the Royal Academy's bad books as their own hired expert, though it would take some doing to explain away why he was stealing a statue he had been engaged to authenticate. And still there remained the tricky, sticky question of why.

"And now, my dear Miss Blois, that I have demonstrated both my ability and my willingness to help ye steal a Verrocchio which ye already own, I should very much like ye to tell me *why* we are stealing such a thing in the first place. It makes damned little sense."

"But I have already told you that I cannot tell you why."

He crossed his arms over his chest. "Not good enough."

She closed her eyes, and turned away. "But I cannot tell you why. I wish I could. I wish a lot of things. But I cannot." She ended on a suspiciously watery sniff.

"Devil take it." His crossed arms seemed to fall of their own accord to his pocket—where he normally kept a handkerchief. "Ye're not going to cry, are ye?"

"No." She shook her head vigorously. "I do not cry. I never cry."

"No one *never* cries." This he knew for a fact.

"I do not. Not even when we had to leave France for the very last time." Her voice faded to a whisper so soft he could hear the catch in her voice.

"Don't. Don't," he ordered again. He was an absolute

idiot when it came to crying females. A quarter of Paris, half of St. Andrews, and all of dockside Leith knew that all he needed was a hiccupy smile and a tale of woe to make him loosen his purse strings. And his breeks. "Please don't cry."

"I will not," she insisted, pinching the bridge of her nose. "I am sorry, but the truth is, I am in a simply awful bit of trouble, and I have got to get out of it, and you are the only disreputable person I know, and I do not know where else to turn."

"Oh, ye're just saying such nice things to soften me up."

"I do not mean to," she sniffed. "I swear."

"But ye have done already." He tried to harden his heart, but the truth was the mortar around his heart—not to mention other, more unruly parts of his anatomy—had already crumbled before sweet, petite, seemingly helpless Miss Blois.

But to tell her so would be deeply imprudent—she might have him stealing the crown jewels next. "Go on back, and change into yer own clothes. We'll take these"—he indicated her second-hand togs—"in a parcel, and then ye'll meet me at the gates of Somerset House tomorrow afternoon, at five PM sharp."

She was so relieved and elated that she threw her arms around his neck, and kissed him soundly on each cheek, in the French manner. And he didn't know when he'd been happier to please anybody.

He allowed himself the infinite pleasure of returning the embrace. Of wrapping his arms tight around her, and holding her close for a moment, no more.

It was harder than he thought to let her go.

He firmed his voice. "And wear something practical. Nothing particular, or personal. Respectable clothes, no more, no less. Cottons, not silk. Plain edgings, no lace. Do ye understand? No jewelry. Nothing that is memorable, or that would cause anyone to look yer way." Which was nearly impossible—she was too beautiful not to be memorable. But he had to try.

She agreed to his strictures without a word of argument.

"Thank you, Mr. Andrews." It was as if she were lit from within, so luminous and grateful was her smile. "I can never thank you enough."

Yes, she could.

He had plans for Mignon Blois that he was sure would astonish her just as much as they had already astonished him.

Chapter 13

THE NEXT DAY at precisely four o'clock in the afternoon, Mignon smoothed her nervous hands over her drab, practical skirts, picked up her well-tied parcel, and tried to firm her shaky resolve.

Now that the time had come, she was not sure she could go through with it. She was not sure she could accompany Mr. Andrews, and play the charwoman, and be a thief.

But she was a Blois, after all, an ancient if dishonorable house full of rogues and scoundrels. Surely she could act as one of them. Surely the spirit of her naked, forgery-posing grandmama would see her through the course she had set for herself.

Not that any nakedness ought to be involved with Mr. Andrews's plan, though she was going to have to change her clothes, after all. But he had always acted as the most gentlemanly of thieves.

And he did seem to have a good, solid, unimpeachable plan. A plan that required her at that moment to take her parcel, and exit her safe, predictable home in Soho Square.

In the foyer, Henri stood ready to open the front door. "Good afternoon, *Mademoiselle du Blois*. Going out?"

"Yes, Henri." Mignon paused, thinking perhaps she ought to say something in case—in case things didn't go according to Mr. Andrews's well-prepared plan. In case she did end the evening in a small dank cell.

Best not to think about that. "Pray tell my father that I will be dining out this evening, and may be out, in fact, quite late, and he need not wait up for me."

Henri was too good a servant to raise his brows at such a hoydenish plan—she had never in her life taken dinner from home without her father—but she could feel and hear Henri's approbation in his restraint. "Very good, *Mademoiselle*. I shall tell *Monsieur le Comte* when he returns. He went out, for a walk, he said. I fear he was quite low, *Mademoiselle Mignon*."

It was a token of Henri's concern that he had let himself lapse into such familiar address. "Yes, I fear so, too, Henri. But pray tell him, if you will, that all will be well. And that I am this moment seeing to the matter of his difficulty."

Henri nodded in his solemn, if not quite believing, manner. "If you say so, *Mademoiselle*."

She did say so. She was quite determined.

Yes. There. She had almost convinced herself.

But before Henri could pull open the door, the brass knocker sounded without.

As she had expected no visitors this afternoon, she was more annoyed than alarmed. Still the interruption had her nervy heart clattering away in her chest like an out of time team of horses—unless that sound of horses was real, and was Mr. Andrews come to collect her instead of meeting her at Somerset House as they had arranged. Best to be sure.

"Pray, unless it is Mr. Andrews come to collect me, please tell whomever it is that I am not at home," she instructed Henri before she hid herself out of sight behind the doorway to the salon, where she could listen while Henri opened the portal.

"Good evening, my lord," was Henri's elegant greeting of the unseen caller.

"The Duke of Bridgewater to see Mamselle Blois," was the response.

Oh, of all the people! Mignon had absolutely no desire to

see the Duke of Bridgewater, and even less to hear him mispronounce her name.

"I am sorry, Your Grace." She could almost hear Henri's deep, respectful bow. "*Mademoiselle du Blois* is not at home."

"Not at home, or not at home to visitors?" She could hear the jolly confidence in His Grace's tone—who refused to see a duke? "Send up my card. She'll see me."

"I am deeply sorry, *Monsieur le Duc*. But *Mademoiselle* is not at home, Your Grace."

There was a minute pause while his grace pondered an imponderable—that she might not actually want to see him—before he spoke. "I'll wait."

No, no, no.

But Henri was already out of his considerable depth, because His Grace had already blustered his way through the salon door behind which she was hiding, and was making himself comfortable in her father's wing chair closest to the hearth.

Which meant she had two choices—she could either stay hidden and hope that he grew too bored, or she could bluster her own way out of—

"Ahh. There she is! Your man said you'd gone out." His Grace of Bridgewater had already spied her, and was on his feet, advancing upon her apace.

"Oh, good evening, Your Grace." Mignon fussed with her skirts and parcel, as if she had had business behind the door. "I am on my way out, but I forgot something." She lifted her carefully wrapped parcel as evidence. "Thank you, Henri, I will show His Grace out on my way."

"No, no," the duke insisted. "Can't go yet. Made up my mind, y'see? Have to do it while the blood's high."

Whatever it was he had to do with his blood high involved clasping her hand in an alarmingly familiar manner.

Mignon attempted to free herself from his unwelcome grasp. "Your Grace, I do not think it is advisable to do anything while the blood is high. You might do yourself a fatal injury."

He did not take her suggestion to heart. Nor did he

surrender her hand. "Fear not. It's only a short speech, don't you know."

"I do not know, but I am afraid I have not got the time to find out. You see—"

But he was already leading her toward the chaise. "Oh, you French girls—not a moment to waste, what? So I shan't waste your time." He clasped her hand in his in that alarmingly familiar fashion, and came right to his point. "I am come so you might do me the honor of making me the happiest man alive."

Mignon felt as if she had stepped too close to a fire—the prickly heat of embarrassment was the same. "Oh," she tried to smile over her confusion, for politeness' sake. "How might I do that, Your Grace?"

"By marrying me, of course."

It was as if he had gifted her with an exotic elephant on a lead line—Mignon did not know when she had been more astonished, or more ill-prepared to accept.

Except every time she had spoken with Mr. Andrews, of course.

But his large grace, the Duke of Bridgewater, was certainly no Mr. Andrews. "Marriage? But we—" She struggled for an excuse. Any excuse. "But I hardly know you, Your Grace."

The duke waved her concern aside. "What does that signify? You know I'm a duke. You'll get to know me. What the engagement's for, what?" He was everything confident and jolly—completely assured of his success.

And she had to disappoint him. And soon. She had an exhibition to burgle. "But I cannot possibly get engaged to a man I have only just met, even a *duc*."

"But you'll be a duchess, m'dear. Thank of that."

As if money and position would solve all her problems. Though they might solve many, they could certainly not solve her most pressing one.

"Yes, but I really must think about that, you see, for I do not know the first thing about being a duchess."

"Your father is a count, is he not?"

"Well, only lately come into that title, as a courtesy"— she scrambled for excuses— "because, well, the aristocracy in France is no more."

"Which is why we must do our best to keep you here. Bring new blood to our sceptered isle, what?"

All she had to offer the poor man was tainted blood. "I am sorry, Your Grace. I am sensible of the honor you do me, but I needs must have a good long time to consider before I can—"

"Well, dukes, and the opportunity to become their duchess, don't grow on trees y'know, what?" He kissed her hand. "Don't take too long, m'dear girl."

Behind him the Sèvres clock on the mantelpiece chimed the half hour. She had only thirty minutes left to get herself to the gates of Somerset House. She'd have to run.

"Why do you not come back tomorrow, Your Grace?" With any luck, might be in a gaol tomorrow. "After I have had a chance to think, and … and talk to my father. I must speak to him, of course, before I may make a decision."

"What a good idea! Let us both speak to him, as I'm sure—"

"No!" The last thing on earth she needed was for her darling, dishonest papa to find a duke dangling at her fingertips—Papa would fill all of Bridgewater House with his forgeries. "It is a very delicate thing with my papa. I am all he has left, you see, from the revolution."

"All he has left, besides his marvelous collection. How can he be alone with all this magnificent art?" The duke made a thorough perusal of the salon walls—walls covered in forged paintings—as if he thought he was the one getting one up on her papa.

Oh, good luck with that—he would need an impossibly long ladder if he ever thought to get one up upon her papa.

But that was not what a duke wanted to hear. "Yes. Quite," was all she could possibly say.

Unfortunately, it was the wrong thing. "I'll take that as a yes!" His grace beamed at her, and patted her hand.

He really was the most trying man. Even more so than

Mr. Andrews.

Who was, no doubt, already waiting for her in the arched gateway of Somerset House. "No, Your Grace, you misunder—"

"Say no more, m'dear mamselle." He kissed her cold hand, and patted it again, as if she were a child, or a particularly obedient and pleasant dog. "You really are just the thing."

"I am not, Your Grace." But the man wasn't really listening, so she had much rather save her breath to cool more porridge, and do the most expedient thing. "You do me a great honor, Your Grace. An honor I must think about very carefully, for I fear that I am not worthy of so great and distinguished and rarefied"—that ought to please him—"an honor. I pray you would give me some time in contemplation and consultation with my dear father, who will no doubt be heartbroken at the thought of losing me."

"Well, yes. But we'll give him other compensations, shall we?"

They most certainly would not.

Because there really was only one thing that was going to compensate and please her dear papa—for her to steal the Verrocchio. And for that, the man she needed was not the Duke of Bridgewater, but a gentleman thief by the name of Mr. Rory Andrews.

Chapter 14

RORY PACED THE length of the deep arched gate at the entrance to Somerset House and back, and still, there was no sign of Miss Blois. And if she did not arrive within the next—he consulted his watch for the hundredth time since he had arrived half an hour ago—two and one half minutes, he was going home. He was certainly not going to steal her precious statue by himself.

Where would be the fun, or gain, in that?

Of course, doing so might impress Miss Blois. And that would be a good thing. But if she didn't have the nerve to come out and help him steal her own damn statue, well, he wasn't sure she really was fit to become the mother of his future children—black-haired, light-fingered imps that they were destined to be.

As he stood grousing and cooling his badly polished heels, out on the Strand a disreputable hackney carriage was rolling to a stop, but before it could do so, its door swung open to disgorge his Miss Blois, who jumped to the pavement at a run, practically throwing coins at the driver in her haste.

"Am I late?" She was breathless, as if she had run the whole of the way from Soho Square instead of only from the carriage. And her eyes, those dark, wide, appealing eyes searched his face as if she had rather have done anything rather than disappoint him.

And he knew, even if that were not true—even if she was simply forgetful and rushed—he knew he would have waited for her into the dark of the evening. He would have waited even if she had not come. And he would have gone and stolen her blasted statue for her.

But she had come, and he was so very glad she had.

It would never do to tell her so. "Aye. Only just." He let his impatience color his voice. "Where on earth have ye been?"

"Getting betrothed."

Rory felt as if his feet had been kicked out from under him. "To whom—if I may be so impertinent as to ask?"

"To a duke." She let out a put-upon sigh, and shook her head as if she might clear it. "It was awful. He showed up—the Duke of Bridgewater, if you please—and he would not listen to a word I spoke, nor stop his talking, and I did not want to be late, so I got engaged to him as a last resort, so I might leave, and come to you. But am I too late?" Her pale brow was flushed that angelic vermillion pink, and pleated up with her distress.

So she wasn't actually betrothed.

Rory regained a little of his *sang froid* at her obvious dislike of being so importuned. Bloody duke. "It's all right. Ye're only just here in time." His own relief was so profound that he had to share it with her. "In fact, the exhibition is open for another fifteen minutes, so if ye'd like to go back and actually marry him, or better yet, refuse him, I suppose I can cool my heels for—"

"Oh, *mon Dieu.* The thought is not to be borne. He only wants me to get to the Verrocchio."

Rory felt a pang of something that must be his conscience. It all came back to the Verrocchio, even for him—They were all trying to get to the statue, though for different reasons.

But the darling lass had linked her arm with his in the most pleasingly familiar fashion, and was hurrying him toward the entrance. "Come, Mr. Andrews. We have not a moment to lose."

They had a great deal more than a moment to lose, both of them—reputation, career, security, liberty. The list was inexhaustible. But still he walked on.

Within Somerset House, a highly fashionable crowd was still milling about, gathering largely near the Diana, which stood in the center of the exhibition space. He steered Miss Blois and her string-wrapped parcel through the throng, again taking note of where the Bow Street Runners who were acting as guards were stationed in doorways and at the corners of the rooms. But they hadn't much time in which to get acclimatized—the hour of reckoning was nigh upon them.

What they needed to start the evening off right was a little disturbance. "Walk by the guard and drop yer parcel," he whispered into her ear.

"Me?" The rosy vermillion faded from her face. "But what if they want to look at the parcel, and they see the old clothes?"

"They won't be looking at the parcel," he assured her. "Just drop it near enough to distract their attention, and while ye're bending to retrieve it, ye'll very likely show a bit of yer well-turned ankles—they're lovely, yer ankles, by the way. So ye might think to use them. Simple, very easy plan."

Her face suffused with that delicious dash of delicate color at the compliment. But this was no time to let himself be distracted by Miss Blois's angelic beauty. There was sleight of hand to be done. "Off ye go." He put his hands to those seemingly fragile, but strong shoulders, and pushed her in the runner's direction.

And damned if she didn't manage it all as well as a veteran actress upon a Drury Lane stage—a little fumble, a cooing sound of embarrassment, an innocent bending over of a shapely bottom, finished off with an elegant show of ankle.

Rory had to take himself firmly in hand, tear his eyes away from the pleasing sight, and do his part. The moment the runner's attention was so brilliantly diverted, Rory dodged behind the ropes dividing the public space from the private, quickly lifted the key from the rack he had located at the back of the stairwell on his previous visit, and unlocked the small door to the broom closet under the stair.

And before Miss Blois had even had a chance to recover her poise, he was back at her side, taking up her parcel and her arm like the most solicitous of swains, and escorting his partner in soon-to-be-crime away to safety. But not before he sent the runner an absolutely filthy look over his shoulder for presuming to ogle her ankles.

Just as he had so clearly required, damn his eyes.

Needs must while the devil drives. "Well done, my dear. And so we are set." He took the precaution of consulting his pocket watch. "With three minutes to spare. Well then, I suppose we have a few minutes left for cultural improvement."

"Three minutes until closing?" she asked. "But what are we going to do then, when the exhibit closes?"

"I am glad ye asked." He steered her toward the entryway. "What we are going to do is not panic. Like this gentleman"—he indicated the large self-portrait of Sir Joshua that graced the entryway—"I am going to rely on the instinct we all have to 'protect what is ours.' Or more precisely, to depreciate that which is *not* truly ours."

She frowned and looked from the portrait of Sir Joshua back to him. "I do not understand."

"Let me demonstrate." He led her on to the next painting—a large Rubens from the Duke of Bridgewater's collection—where a runner stood. "Is this Dutch?" he asked the chap.

The liveried runner curled up his lip, and shrugged with supreme indifference. "Dunno, gov."

"Ah, thank you." Rory moved on to the next painting. "Ye see, all this terribly nice and terribly expensive artwork is not his. And without a profit motive, like there is with thief-taking, the runner will be paid whether he guards this priceless Holbein *Still Life with Pheasant*, or some other painting of a meal he will not eat."

"Oh, I see." She looked up at him with something perilously close to respect. "A little."

"Then let me explain further." He indulged himself with the feel of the warmth of her sleeve under his fingertips as he led her on to another painting. "The nice thing about complicated mechanical devices, such as specially made, alarmed locks"—he circumscribed the air in front of the painting as if he were discussing the merits of Caravaggio's opulent rendering of fruit—"is that very few people know exactly how to use them. And when they go off, these alarms, especially for the first time, everyone gets a fright, and everything goes to hell in a hand cart. And that is when we shall take our ride."

Just saying the words brought a tingle to his palms and a pleasurable tightness to his chest.

And she felt it, too—that anticipatory rush of excitement. Her mouth fell open just a tad—just enough for the very tip of her tongue to dart out to wet her plush lower lip—and it was everything he could do not to take her heart-shaped face in his hands, and kiss her with everything he had in him.

But now was not the time. Later, perhaps.

Later, definitely.

"Ah!" he exclaimed as they came to the next painting, very near to the large fireplace. "Superb Raphaelo." He consulted his watch again, and found the hour was nigh. "Now, Miss Blois, we have reached what we may safely call the point of no return. In precisely one minute, the closing gong will sound, and we can be logical, and leave with the others, and go have quiet dinner *chez moi*. Or we stay, and then we are well and truly committed. From that point there can be no going back. But before we do one or the other, ye have to decide if ye really want the statue that much—if ye are truly willing to risk everything ye have, everything ye are."

She did not hesitate. "*À tout prix.*" She nodded, even as she bit her lip. "I am, at any price. I must do it." She pulled a shaky breath into her lungs, expanding her chest beneath the filmy cover of her modest linen fichu. "But you do have a plan that you think is going to work, do you not? You are not just—"

"I think it will work. Yes. I am confident." Lord, he hoped so, or he would have a lot of explaining to do. Not that he wouldn't have a great deal of explaining to do no matter what happened, but he was prepared for all eventualities. "If ye're sure?"

She nodded again, stepping infinitesimally closer. Putting herself into his care.

Rory felt his own lungs expand with that addictive tingle of anticipation and excitement. "I put myself in yer charge." He eyed the position of the runners one last time. "Just do exactly as I tell ye."

And then the gong was going off—one of the runners wound his way through the whole of the exhibition rooms ringing out the time—and everything changed.

Everyone started to race slowly, like tortoises, toward the entrance door. Everything sped up and slowed down. Everything sounded louder, and more muted. Everything narrowed to the feel of his hand on the perfect curve that was the small of her back as he guided her into place beside the chimney piece, and the rest of the runners started herding the visitors toward the doors, picking up pieces of litter and discarded exhibition sheets as they went.

Before the runners came nearer to where they stood, Rory pulled out the handkerchief he had prepared with a handful of coins carefully folded into the center, and propped it negligently, just so, on top of his exhibition program, on the corner of the marble-topped credenza upon which a small bronze cherub figure was displayed.

He turned his back and moved slowly away, smiling at Mignon to keep her attention focused on him, and not on what was about to happen behind him. For just as he had hoped, the runner tried to brush the litter into his wicker bin, causing the hidden cache of coins to spill from the handkerchief, and cascade across the floor. And just as he had hoped, the runners scrabbled after the coins, grubbing around on hands and knees, while he put his hand on top of Miss Blois's neat little black hat, and stuffed her down behind the tapestry screen, and into the deep recess of the fireplace.

Rory waited only another moment to check to make sure the runners' attention was still diverted, before he slipped in beside her, turning his black-clad back to the mouth of the fireplace, and wrapping his arms around her.

Within the close confines of the sooty smelling space, there was nothing but their warm, co-mingled breath, and the taut press of Miss Blois's sweetly rounded hip against his thigh.

Lucky damn thigh.

But he couldn't simply lose himself to the pleasure of her closeness, all curled up beside him—he had to listen carefully to the retreating footfalls, and auger the exact moment when the runners had vacated the room.

When there was nothing but silence filling the exhibition space, Rory cautiously raised his head over the fire screen, to find the coast was clear, and then he hustled her up and out of the fireplace, and down to the small, unlocked broom closet under the stairs. Which had just about enough room for half of him. Poor Miss Blois was practically plastered right up against the whole length of his body, from torso to toes.

It was quite perfect for his purposes.

"Comfy?" he whispered, as he silently shut them in.

"No. I mean…" Her whisper was a little frayed at the edges. "I had not thought it would be quite so…close. Or dark. I do not like closed spaces."

He tried to charm away her discomfort. "My apologies. It's a sad crush, but what can one do? We'll pretend we're at an overcrowded soiree. If ye just give me a moment…"

He shifted his position just enough so that the thin line of light from under the bottom of the door gave them some illumination by which to reach into his rather copious pockets, and produce a very small, portable, shuttered lantern favored by housebreakers. "This is what's known in the trade as a 'glim,'" he explained as he knelt down. "If ye could watch yer skirts while I light it?"

"You must have the eyes of the cat." He waited through a supremely pleasurable interlude while fabric shushed and whispered against his face, as she pulled her shirts and petticoats aside. "Will that do?"

He, of course, had to run his hand from her tiny feet up across those marvelously trim ankles to the top of her stockinged shins. For safety's sake.

"That will do nicely." It took some doing to strike the flint against the oil-impregnated wool wick, but in another moment or two the small lamp was glowing, and they could take stock of their close confines. The closet held an assortment of brooms, mops, and pails for the char women. There was barely room for the two of them to stand chest to chest, and Rory had to stoop so as not to bash his head against the low ceiling. But if they sat, there would be more room in the low, sloping portion that ran under the stairs.

Miss Blois— No, Mignon—it was beyond ridiculous to stand on formalities when he couldn't even stand. Mignon had followed the dim light on its cursory inspection of the space, but then looked to him, her eyes wide and dark with something more than mere discomfort.

Some instinct he hadn't known he possessed had him wrapping his arm lightly around her back, but even under the guise of comfort, Rory could feel her shallow breathing and erratic pulse practically leaping through the intervening layers of their clothes.

"We'll get more comfortable in a little while," he assured her in a low murmur against the delicate whorl of her ear. "After the initial danger passes."

"Danger?" There was more than tension in her voice— there was something dangerously close to irrational panic.

"Of being discovered."

He heard her quick gasp, but the moment was already upon them—footsteps were approaching. "Hush, now." He doused the glim, and in the pressing darkness Mignon Blois quite naturally clung to him, putting her hands and face against his chest as the sound of the footfalls grew louder.

Rory did the manful thing and held her tight while whispering sweet comforting nothings into her ear. For her sake, of course—she was practically shaking with fear. Especially when the heavy tread could be heard around the back of the stair. And then closer, at the very door to the closet.

And the moment he heard the metallic snick of the latch, Rory did the logical, expedient, and entirely practical thing, and kissed her.

Chapter 15

HIS MOUTH COVERED hers.

Mignon was too astonished and too afraid to make a sound, though she had never in her life been kissed the way Mr. Andrews was kissing her now, with his whole mouth on hers. With his whole being. Deeply. Intimately. Madly.

She had seen them on the streets here in London, as well as in Paris—the couples entwined in each other's' arms and oblivious to all but the press of their lover's lips—but she had never expected to become one of them.

But it felt rather nice and warm and interesting and somehow safe to be held so by Rory Andrews. In his arms, the panic of the dark ebbed, and something far more pleasurable flowed in to take its place.

Because his kiss made her want to close her eyes, the better to feel the extraordinary experience of his mouth on hers. To feel the smooth tautness of his lips, like the fruit of a pomegranate, firm and giving. He kissed gently at first, moving his lips slightly against hers, waiting for her to grow accustomed to the intimacy. Waiting for her to take part. With her whole being.

She could not have said why she did so, but something—something stronger than curiosity and weaker than the fear—compelled her to wrap her arms around his neck to hold him close, and press her lips to his. To let him slide his hands across her back, over her shoulders and up the length of her neck to cradle her jaw, and turn her head ever so slightly, like some strange personal jigsaw puzzle. Because the moment he tipped her head to the side, it was as if she fit him. As if they fit together even more closely.

A tension that was something different from panic started low in her belly and worked outward through her body, until every inch of her felt alive and moving of its own accord. Moving into the kiss. Into him, until there was no space left between them. Becoming almost one.

His kisses reminded her that she was not alone. That whatever terrors remained to be faced, he would face with her. That he had pledged himself to her aid, and would hold himself to her service in more ways than one.

And with that knowledge the darkness receded, and was replaced by the bright light of pleasure. And growing passion.

She gave herself up to the kiss, to learning first the texture and then the taste of him—cinnamon and brandy, heady and warm, exotic and intoxicating. Her head spun, as if she had drunk too much sherry. But oh, such a lovely feeling. So very, very pleasurable. A kiss so gentle and sweet and stealthy it stole her breath, and was well on the way toward stealing her heart when he eased his lips from hers.

"The guard"—he punctuated the information with a kiss to the tip of her nose—"has gone. And the lights"—another kiss first to one closed eye, and then to the other—"have been put out." He pressed a lingering kiss to her lips. "And my plan for us to appear like two lovers who found an out of the way spot to kiss is no longer needed. But I've afraid while we were more pleasantly engaged, he's locked us in."

Locked in.

His voice was everything calm and even amused, but without his kiss to distract her, the air immediately felt hot and thin, and the walls too close. "*Non, non. Je suis à bout de souffle.*" She tried to push her way to the door, to give herself space. "Please. I have to leave."

Her voice sounded small and wretchedly weak, even to her own ears, but she had to make him understand the hot press of panic beating in her ears. It was as if she could hear the dull roar of the mob outside her uncle's house in Paris, and feel the house shake and windows shatter as bricks and cobbles smashed against it. If Papa had not heard her screams, and pulled her from the locked armoire where the treacherous maids had shut her in, she might have—

"Shh. Ye're not out of air," Mr. Andrews assured her. "Ye're fine. I've got ye safe. Just breathe."

She was not fine, but she was not alone. And she was no longer in that armoire in Paris. They had escaped, she and Papa, and fled to London, like rats abandoning a sinking ship. And she was in a closet in London because she had a job to do, a task to accomplish.

The cool air flowed back into her lungs, and with it came logic and sanity. "You understood me," she realized. "You speak French?"

"*Mais oui.*" His voice was all calm breezy assurance. "I lived there, in Paris, for several years as a young man. I know it as well as I know London. Actually, better." His hand resumed its gentle path across her back. "Keep breathing. Ye're just fine. I've got ye," he said again.

And he did have her. His arms were all around her, rubbing her back, warming her arms, distracting her from her predicament by running his thumb gently along her lip in a way that made her forget Paris and Papa and closets and rats.

In a way that made her want to draw the flesh of that thumb into her mouth, and bite ever so gently down upon it to taste his skin.

Good Lord above. What an idea.

But Mr. Rory Andrews did not seem to think it was a bad idea. He seemed to think kissing and biting gently was a marvelous, marvelous thing. "Shh," he said as his lips brushed against hers, and his hands slid up to cup her chin. "It will all be fine," he murmured, as one hand delved into her hair, cradling her skull, tugging on the strands and scattering pins. Drawing her in. Relaxing and distracting her from her panic. Protecting and reassuring her, certainly, but also making her aware of him as a very tall, very well built young man. A very gentlemanly gentleman thief.

Ah, yes. Best to remember that he was a thief. And that they were in a broom closet in Somerset House because she needed him to steal her father's statue back to keep Papa from gaol, and her from having to emigrate in shame to America.

"And we're not really locked in—we can leave at any time."

"Truly?" His reassurance pushed the walls back, and his lovely strong fingers were smoothing along the tight lines of her shoulders, and gently kneading the tense muscles of her upper back. And it felt quite heavenly to rest there for the moment, with her head against his chest.

"Yes, truly," he concurred. "But it's best we wait another moment or two." His voice was a low hum that vibrated though her, tickling her in the most strangely un-annoying way, making her bones feel soft and pliable. "Lily of the valley," he observed in an easy, lazy murmur, as if he were reciting a recipe, or an incantation. "From Houbigant on the Rue Faubourg Saint-Honoré. I would know that scent anywhere. How quintessentially French. And delightful. Like ye."

It was a good thing the closet was dark, or he would see the furious blush heating her cheeks. Because he was still holding her, still slowly drawing his fingers through her hair in that calming fashion, so she did not leave his embrace. Nor remove her head from where it lay so comfortably against the safe wall of his chest.

"I understand." His lovely articulate fingers played along the nape of her neck, distracting and soothing her all at the same time. "Why don't we try to sit? I'll go first."

He disengaged his arms from their embrace, and immediately she felt the loss of him—the loss of calm and comfort. But he did not leave her entirely—not that he could in so tight a space—he took her hand, and interlaced his strong fingers through her smaller ones until he could pull her down upon his lap. "More comfortable?" he asked as his arm resumed drawing lazy circles in the small of her back.

"Will I not squash you?"

"Not a'tall. I'm perfectly comfortable." His low, easy voice betrayed not a qualm. "There's room for my legs to be stretched out under the stair, and ye weigh no more than a featherweight. Or a very lovely paperweight." He placed another kiss unerringly upon her brow. "Ye might as well lean on me. We need to rest while we can."

And then he un-shuttered the glim, as he called the small lantern she had not heard him retrieve from the shelf, and silently louvered the tiny doors open enough that the warm, mellow wick illuminated their close confines.

"Does that make it better, or worse?"

"Better I think." Because she could see him, and see the contented smile he lavished upon her at close range.

"I suppose you must think me silly to be afraid in the dark. I did not used to be. But things, before, in Paris—" She struggled to explain something she had no right to complain about. She and Papa were alive and well, when so many others were not.

"Things in Paris got complicated," he offered, "and dark."

"Yes. Just so." It was an inordinate relief to be understood without the necessity of explanation, or of translation. Her gentleman thief had intriguing depths.

"And so we will keep things as simple and uncomplicated as possible," he assured her.

"But what can be done about the lock?"

"Oh, I have plans for that lock when the time comes, don't ye worry. Do ye know what someone once told me?"

"No." She hadn't the vaguest idea, because his clever fingers were working their way up the column of her spine, and were tracing soft circles just below her hairline in a way that made her want to tip her head back to give him greater access. Even though she knew perfectly well that she ought not. She ought to concentrate upon their problem, and help him where she could.

But he seemed to have everything so well in hand, as it were. And he was murmuring, "A friend once told me that old locks are like maiden aunties—they know how to keep their secrets, so ye have to cozen up to them sweetly."

"Is that what you are doing to me—cozening up to me sweetly?"

"Is it working?" he asked at the edge of her ear.

"A little," she admitted.

He smiled, a slow spark that lit in one corner of his eye and spread. "Then I'll have to try harder."

But he really didn't try harder—he tried sweeter. He kissed her sweetly. More than sweetly. Heartwarmingly gently. He kissed like an angel, if angels were tall and terrible and handsome, with the most astonishingly translucent blue eyes that went soft at the corners when he looked at her.

His hand wrapped around the back of her neck, and his fingers splayed along the line of her jaw to tip her face up to his. To fit them together like two halves of a puzzle she hadn't known she needed to solve. His lips pressed against hers, gently but insistently, telling her without words that he wanted more from her. More of her mouth. More of her lips. More of her tongue.

His own tongue licked subtly at the corner of her mouth—just enough. Just enough to make her lips part, and make her gasp with astonishment at the abiding sweetness that rose within her as he took her lower lip between his, and softly sucked and worried at her flesh.

She opened to him then, wanting everything of pleasure he had to give, needing more and more of the slippery friction of his mouth upon hers. Her eyes fell closed, and her head fell back. His mouth slid down to the side of her neck, where he worried and nipped against the sensitive tendon.

Oh, *Bon Dieu*, he was good at this.

"You must do this sort of thing all the time." Her fingers found a button upon his coat—a crest of some sort—and fiddled with it idly.

"Not all the time." He kissed in between the words. "I'm very selective, ye ken—I rob only the best, most interesting people, with the loveliest, most interesting daughters."

"Many daughters?"

His answer was to kiss the side of her neck. "As a matter of fact, ye're my first." His mouth slid along the line of her jaw, and pleasure weighted her head. "Normally, I don't get myself apprehended by lovely young women in their night clothes, or cozied up in a closet with them."

"Do you often work with other thieves, when you work?"

"Never. Ye're my first accomplice, and therefore also my best."

She tried not to be pleased, not to smile, so she hid her chagrin by finding his lips—those lovely, strong, firm, clever lips, that kissed her in a way that made her forget about closets, and think instead of night clothes, and how she wished she were not wearing so many layers of clothes right now so she might feel the touch of his hand more directly.

And perhaps he felt the same way, because he was untying his cravat, and opening his collar, allowing her to find the hollow at the base of his throat, and kiss him there. His skin was smooth and warm and smelled of citrus and bright sunlight. "Limes," she murmured, "from Floris, on Jermyn Street. So very, very"—she punctuated her discovery with kisses—"quintessentially"—another kiss that was more of a taste of his taut flesh—"exotically English."

"No one,"—he made quick work of her plain linen fichu—"has ever called the English exotic. And I'm Scots."

"Oh, you are," she assured him. "English or British—it is all the same, is it not? Then you are so very, wonderfully British."

"As ye are so French. *Si belle*. So lovely." His fingers skimmed across her skin. "*Si douce*. So soft."

With him, she did not mind being French. She did not mind being locked in a closet. She did not even mind being a thief.

Because in return, he have her more of the heady, intoxicating pleasure, heating and cooling her skin, making her forget everything except him, and his mouth, and the infinite possibility of pleasure.

Until he disappointed her, and said, "Oh, Mignon. Please, we must stop."

Chapter 16

"FORGIVE ME A moment."

Mignon opened her eyes to find him checking the time on his pocket watch.

"It's about a minute before nine o'clock, when the guards should make their first rounds. And they may check this closet. And being caught out as trysting lovers doesn't suit my plans so well now. So I think it best we reposition ourselves where we can't be seen, and squash up there"—he nodded his head at the dark low space at his feet—"under the stair."

Perhaps he felt the instinctive shiver of anticipatory dread that sketched across her skin, or perhaps she bit down on her lip the way she always did when she had to do something she didn't like, but either way, he very kindly tried his best to ease her way.

"Now, this, I reckoned, might be a problem." He chatted in that calm, matter-of-fact way he had when he had been attempting to rob her—all breezy charm. "Because it will be tight and close—even tighter and closer than already. But strangely enough, the thing I want now, more than anything else in the world, is to be closer to ye. To lie down with ye in my arms, and hold ye tight. And kiss ye senseless. And have ye kiss me silly."

When he put it like that, it didn't seem daunting, or frightening at all. It seemed like a wonderful idea. Because what she wanted more than anything else in the world was to be closer to him.

And he was already kissing her senseless, because she didn't seem to feel any distress in the least when he laid her down in his arms, and pressed her up tight against his chest with his legs tangled in her skirts.

"So soft." His breath fanned across her skin, as he kissed across her temples. "So sweet. So beautiful."

She felt beautiful, even though she knew he could not see her. She felt soft and sweet and carefree with his lips on her skin. She felt warm and safe and wonderful, and she wanted to burrow into the lean strength of his chest and keep herself there. The dark pressed in around her, impelling her into his arms. Impelling her to feel. And taste. And dream.

"Mignon," he whispered, as if it were an invitation.

And invitation she wanted to immediately accept. She did not know how wonderful, how pleasing her name would sound on his lips. "Yes," was all she could think to answer. Yes, she was there. Yes, she wanted the lovely feelings he was creating in her body with his hands and his mouth and his tongue. Yes, she wanted more.

She gave him that answer with her lips on his, tasting the salt tang of his skin, feeling the rapid pulse of his heartbeat under the surface, hearing the way his breathing changed when she gave into the temptation she had felt earlier, and put her teeth to his neck, and bit down ever so gently while she poured her fingers through his hair, disrupting the smooth queue. Tugging him closer. Holding him still.

He kissed her back with the same growing ferocity, the same need and heat and passion, and nothing else existed. Nothing but his warmth and his texture and his fresh clean scent enveloping her, holding her together and pushing her apart, and always, always making her feel safe.

He pulled her flush against the length of his body, his lovely large hand spanning the small of her back, and she fitted herself to him, pliant and accommodating, filling the last breath of space between them. His other hand was at her nape, cradling her head, angling her jaw so he could take her mouth, and fill her longing with the sweep of his tongue.

Warmth spread throughout her body, covering her like a blanket, soft and secure.

Mignon closed her mind to all other thoughts and concentrated only on the feelings dissolving along the surface of her skin, on the pleasure sinking into her bones.

Beneath the layers of clothes her body grew restless and dissatisfied by the constraints of fabric and fashion. Her breasts grew sensitive and tender, longing for his touch. And his hand was there, skimming up the side of her stays, sliding over the intervening layers of fabric, easing her need with the warm weight of his palm.

She arched into his hand, angling her body to appease the low ache that began deep in her belly and spread outward until it reached the surface of her skin. Her breath came fast, but she didn't need air—she only needed him, and his hand and his care and the pleasure that was almost pain.

"Mignon," he said again. "My Sweet Mignon. We must stop."

"No." She heard the disappointment in her whisper, and could not seem to make herself ease her grip upon his neck and his lapel. "Not now. Not when—"

"We must. For now. We must be quiet." There was promise enough in his words that she objected no further when he laid his finger across her lips, and whispered. "Hold tight."

She heard it then—the tramp of the guards as they stomped out from their room at the back of the gallery. Closer and closer they drew, and Mignon practically held her breath as a heavy footfall sounded upon the stair mere inches above their heads.

If she had been able to move she would have clamped her palms over her ears so she might try to block it all out.

But he blocked it out. By quietly, silently, stealthily kissing her once more, by sinking his fingers deep into her hair, cradling her skull and holding her tight, until there was nothing but him, and his lips and his breath.

And want. Growing, unfathomable want.

And she definitely wanted more.

But he was edging his way backward out of the space, and opening the glim to check his watch. "That took about three minutes from start to finish. And they came out just after the turn of the hour, so they're not exactly chomping at the bit. Good to know."

It was also good to know that Rory Andrews could still think and kiss. Unlike her, who had been lost to everything but the comfort and distraction he offered. Surely this must be her tainted blood rushing to the fore, this liking ruinous behavior. "I do not know what came over me."

His smile started in one corner of his eye and spread, like English marmalade, all across his face. "I rather think it was me that came over ye. But next time, perhaps ye will want to come over me. I think I should like that."

"Next time?"

"Oh, yes. Next time. We've got a very long night ahead of us, my Mignon, and I mean to make the most of it. I hope ye do, too."

"We are still going to steal the statue at the end?"

"Oh, yes, but let's see if we can steal a little something else while we're at it." He pulled her back into his arms. "Perhaps not yer virtue"—he raised his eyebrows to show her he was joking, a little—"but perhaps maybe a tiny little piece of yer heart. But really, it's more like to be a not-so-tiny piece of my heart."

He let go of her to angle the glim more to his liking. "And this time, I should like to see ye. To look at ye and see the beauty that feels and tastes so fine. I should like to see how my kisses make ye feel."

This time she did not mind the flush of color that was surely racing across her skin, because he followed it with his fingertips, painting sensation on top of warmth. Making awareness seep deep under her skin, soaking into her bones.

She melted into him, into his warmth and surety and light. Into his care.

Mignon gave him a soft, happy sigh of capitulation when he covered her fingers with his lovely long, lean hands. His fingers were beautifully articulated—aristocratic, she would have said, had she not known better—and covered her smaller hands completely. But they were as gentle as they were strong—though he held her lightly, she could feel his strength of his muscle and bone.

"Do ye like that?" he asked quietly. "The way it feels—the heat and fit—when our palms touch? The way I am making ye feel?"

Mignon nodded her answer, afraid she would not have the right English words to describe the strange combination of lust and trust brewing within like a potent *tisane*.

"Good." He smiled that smile that was all in the corners of his eyes, soft and drowsy, and spread their hands wide, before he dropped then gently at her side. He left her hands to their own devices while he placed his palms softly on either side of her neck. His thumbs grazed along the line of her jaw, but just when she thought he would pull her close and kiss her, he did the opposite. He leaned her back into the wall opposite. "So I can look at ye."

Mignon found her breath coming fast and shallow against the tight binding of her stays, and within, under the layers of lacing and linen, her breasts grew tight and heavy, and she felt as warm and quivery as a custard, waiting for his touch.

The quivering intensified when his thumb slipped along the sensitive line of her collarbone. Mignon held herself still, the better to feel the rush of anticipatory sensation race across the surface of her skin like a hot wind across the water.

He pressed a hot kiss to the hollow of her neck, and she closed her eyes to better concentrate, to feel every feeling at its most intense. His soft, sandy hair brushed against her chin and jaw, tickling her, making her spear her fingers through the silky slide of his warm locks. Holding his head, and tethering him to her, so he would kiss her there, where her breasts were tight and full and aching with need.

He kissed along to the curve of her shoulder, wetting the skin, before he began to peel back the fabric from her shoulder, pushing her bodice down incrementally to expose the bare rounds of her shoulders, and the soft tops of her breasts.

His touch was feather light and exquisite, careful, as if she were delicate or fragile, but sure, sending shivers of pleasure streaking under the surface of her skin. He stroked up the side of her neck to her nape, and she tilted her head into his hands, wanting more of the breath-stealing sensations, offering herself up to the attention of his left, which he turned so he could trail the backs of his fingers across the flushed flesh at the very edge of her bodice.

Once, twice. Back and forth he stroked, lightly, so lightly, until she was arching toward him, pulling the fabric down with her own hands to expose the ruched peaks of her breasts.

"Mignon," was all he said, but his voice was a combination of delight and wonder that filled her with something more than mere pleasure. More than anticipation.

With want.

And he did not disappoint. He swooped down to cover the pink tips with his lips, kissing her with exquisite skill. She fisted her hands in his hair, holding him to her, wanting more of the need that spiraled deep within. She felt tight and full and unsatisfied, because she was sure there was something more, something that would appease the needy hunger growing within in a way that all his kisses could not.

And then she could not say if it was she or he who grappled closer—but they were kissing, lip to mouth, fierce and purposeful, holding nothing back. He kissed her with heat and passion, with tongue and teeth and lips, and a hunger she was beginning to understand was want.

And oh, how she wanted. How she wanted this tall, dangerous, elegant English man.

Who pulled away from her, gasping for breath just like she. "My God, Mignon. Ye make me lose my head. We must stop. We must stop before I can no longer call myself a gentleman. Before I completely forget what it was we came here to do."

"To steal," she reminded him. "Stealing a little piece of my heart, along with my Verrocchio."

There must have been something funny in the English words that she did not yet understand, because he began to laugh, and pulled her close to plant a kiss in the middle of her forehead, before he set her away. "We must put ye to rights."

He pulled her sleeves back onto her shoulders in an attempt to set her clothing to some semblance of order. She did the same for him, pulling his collar straight, and smoothing his lapels. It was all so domestic and intimate and easy it was almost frightening.

Frightening because her mind was already casting itself into the future, wondering if it would be like this to wake up next to him every morning. To lie on a bed with him every night.

She had to shake herself to remember other, more pressing fears. "Are we still locked in?"

"Aye. However, it's a very good thing ye brought along a thief, because I have a simple remedy for that." He shook his hair out of his eyes, and then produced a pair of sharp, wicked looking pieces of pointed metal from his waistcoat. "Picklocks."

She could not hide her astonishment. "Do you always keep a set of picklocks hidden in your extraordinarily well-tailored clothes, or is this occasion special?" There had been no rumple or bulge in the smooth flaring seams to indicate otherwise. He certainly had a talented, and discreet, tailor.

"Everything about this occasion is special. But one must always plan for contingencies." He flipped up the tail of his coat with a flourish worthy of a magician performing tricks to reveal a second hidden pocket. "So I have not one, but two."

Her astonishment became admiration. "Well, I will say this for the criminal class—at least you are prepared."

"Didn't learn it from the criminal classes. Quite the opposite. Picking locks was the only useful skill I ever learned at school." He applied the two probes to the keyhole with the precision of a surgeon letting blood from a particular vein, and in no time at all the latch on the door quietly snicked open. "There. It's too early to go out, but just for the fresh air." He pushed the door open enough to reveal the dark emptiness of the exhibition spaces. "Better?"

She took a deep breath of the cooler air. "Much, thank you."

"Ye're most welcome. But now that we have a bit of space, it's time for ye to get changed." He dropped his voice to a low, intimate whisper. "So let's go ahead and get that dress off of ye."

Chapter 17

FOR A LONG moment, Rory thought he had finally succeeded in saying exactly the wrong thing.

And then Mignon lowered her chin, and smiled. "From a man who speaks French and lived in Paris, I had hoped for a little more *finesse.*"

And just like that, he was done in. "Let me rephrase, *chère Mademoiselle.*" Rory kept his voice low, in case the emptiness of the exhibition rooms should make their voices carry. "We will both need to change—ye into yer jumps and quilted petticoat, and me into my livery—before the runners come out for their next round of checks. And I would be honored to assist ye."

She presented him with her back. "Would you—" She blushed, and exquisite swath of madder red painted across her cheeks. "Would you apply your honor to the laces?"

"I had much rather apply my lips." He had to dredge his voice up from somewhere deep within. "But that would not be of the necessary assistance to ye. So I will settle for using my hands."

His normally clever fingers faltered only momentarily, but soon enough he was undoing the simple gown he had so recently done up. And it was going to take all his considerable self-possession to help her unclothe, and leave it at that. Because they needed to stay on schedule, despite all inducements to the contrary. And they were severe inducements.

The inducement of her softly scented skin. And her soft sighs. And her angelically trim little body. And the invitation she was clearly giving him out of the corners of her wide, dark eyes, even if she didn't entirely understand just exactly the extent of that invitation.

The invitation he was going to accept. Someday.

But not today. Not in the middle of a very small closet, in the midst of a very large burglary. Which might go to hell in a hand cart any minute.

But still, he had to kiss the soft spot along her spine where her stays and chemise gave way to sweet skin. And the even softer spot just at the side of her nape. And the sweeter spot under her ear.

And then he set her away, though the plain gown gaped temptingly.

She received this tacit command with a sigh. "I suppose we must stick to the matter at hand, and retrieve the parcel."

He did so, pulling the brown paper package out from the spot where he had stuffed it under the stair, and then fishing his small dirk out of his cuff, and quickly slicing through the string.

"What else have you got in those pockets of yours? Besides picklocks and knives?"

"All manner of bits and bobs." He pulled out the stub of a candle as evidence. "It's just the thrifty Scot in me."

"You said that before." She smiled and frowned all at the same time—it was perfectly calibrated to enchant. "So that is different from being English? But you don't sound different. I can understand everything you say."

Rory had to work to stifle his laugh. "Had the roughest edges of the Scots burr rather forcefully schooled out of me."

"That does not sound pleasant."

"It wasn't. But it got me where I am. Which is with a beautiful young woman this evening."

"In the middle of a burglary."

"Aye." He still smiled at her. "We had best get to it."

Mignon carefully shook out the clothing. "Shall I leave on my chemise and stays? Or—"

"Aye. I mean, leave them on." Suddenly the closet felt too small and too warm for him. "Or we'll never get to the statue." He took a deep, fortifying breath to clear his head of all thoughts of her stays sliding to the floor to pool at her feet along with the gown. "Ye stay here—there is room enough with only one of us—and do yer best with the charwoman's clothes, while I will be back in a moment. I'm going to shut the door," he warned her. "But it won't be locked. Just try to be as quiet as may be."

He left her to dress, and nimbled off, tip-toeing around the passage at the back of the stairwell to retrieve the key to the small closet on the other side. From which he procured a suit of striking livery with the requisite red and white cording, and into which he changed in the dark confines of the passage.

No sooner was he done attaching the eye hooks over the waistcoat, than Mignon cautiously peeped out from the closet, and gasped when she saw him, looming in the shadows.

"It's just me," he assured her as best he could in a whisper. "Though I do not wear a wig. I am hoping they will leave them off at night, when they are off duty to some extent, and out of the public eye."

"Where did you find the coat?" she mouthed.

"Right through that wall." He pointed through the interior of the closet. "Guard's storage. It's as full of livery as this one is of mops and brooms. And speaking of which, we had best get ourselves back inside."

He passed her the neat bundle he had made of his black wool superfine.

"What are we to do with our clothes?" she asked.

"Yer dress, I should think, will fill the bottom of this pail quite nicely"—he demonstrated by pooling the grey poplin in the bucket, where it would make a perfect nest for receiving the Diana—"but I shall unfortunately have to abandon mine."

Understanding lit her face. "Which is why you had such strictures for what to wear. Which I followed, though I felt quite naked coming out without so much as ear bobs."

At the word naked, Rory's mind exercised itself with visions of her just so, clad only in the vermillion pink of her blushes as she lay herself before him, while and demure, and all together nak—

"Rory? Are you quite all to rights?"

"Aye, what? Well done," he babbled to cover both his inattention.

"But I haven't done anything." Her voice was only slightly chiding.

"Ye've done everything right so far."

"Thank you." She tucked her chin to smile. "I suppose it is rather exciting, in a mundane way."

"Let us hope it stays mundane—that is how we'll know we're succeeding."

"Oh. Very good." She seemed to relax a tad. "Then what next?"

"We wait."

"For what exactly?"

"For a little while longer." He gave her his most charming smile so she would know that he was teasing her only half as much as he was teasing himself with naked thoughts of her. But since they had some time before the next scene in their little burglary of a play, they might as well enjoy themselves, at least as much as they had been going before they changed into their present costumes. "Until we get the details right. Yer fichu for instance"—he pointed to the fine linen kerchief still modestly covering her bosom—"is far too fine, and far too modest for a charwoman."

"Is it really?" she asked, but her nimble little fingers were already untucking the kerchief, uncovering an absolutely divine swath of skin so smooth and white and fine it was everything he could do to keep from simply letting his head drop into the shadow between her perfect little breasts.

"Into the bucket with it?"

"Aye." And though he would have been happy to perform the duty for her, he was glad that he had no excuse to bend down along the length of her body. There was no way he could have done it and still remained a gentleman.

As it was, it was hard enough to keep his eyes from the lovely expanse of skin and bosom rising out of the top of her tatty old quilted jumps. "On second thought, perhaps we ought to cover ye up. There is no way that a person as lovely as ye is going to be able to escape the regard of the runners."

"Come now. I am going to be bent over a bucket, am I not? A bucket concealing the statue? At least if the runners are looking at the tops of my bosom, they will not be looking elsewhere."

Her logic was sound. And he was deeply appreciative of how well her mind worked in figuring out some of the details he had yet to tell her. "Clever lass. And very good thinking. Though I dislike intensely the idea that any other man should ogle ye in so callow a manner."

"As opposed to the way you yourself are ogling me now?"

He liked her rather French directness. "Entirely unlike the way in which I am regarding ye now, which is a look filled with reverence of yer person, and awe of yer beauty."

"And will your reverence keep you from trying to kiss me again?"

"Nay," he said immediately. "It will not."

This time when he bent his lips to hers, he did not hold back. He kissed her with everything that he had held in check all evening—all the lust and longing bottled up behind gentlemanly behavior, behind reverence and awe. But along with the reverence and awe was heat and need and something just a step past civilized to be altogether nice.

He kissed her with heat and all of his pent-up passion, backing her against the wall where he could lean his weight into her, and ease some of the hunger growling its way out of his chest.

And she was kissing him back, opening her sweet little mouth, wrapping her arms about his neck, and pressing those luscious little breasts of hers against his chest. They kissed and kissed, tangling tongues, tasting, biting and sucking at each other with hedonistic abandon until all he could think of was putting his hands to her jumps, and lowering her bodice so he might put his mouth, if not his hands, to what he was sure would prove to be the delicate pink whorl of her nipple.

But he did not. He was a gentleman—albeit a gentleman thief for the evening, but a gentleman still. And he wanted more from Mignon Blois than a tumble in a dark closet while he was recovering her father's artwork.

He pulled back, gasping for air, and shoving his fingers deep into his own hair to dispel the itchy need to fill his hands with her flesh. "We ought"—he struggled to get his breath back—"That is to say, *I* really ought keep track of the time."

He made a show of consulting his pocket watch, though it took him more than a few seconds to get his brain to work properly enough to read the time. "They'll be out again in twenty minutes or so, but we'll need to surprise them before that."

"Surprise them how?"

"By setting off the alarms."

Alarm was exactly what showed on her face—her dark eyes went wide with it. "But I would think that would be the last thing you would want to do."

"Not necessarily. Remember that runner earlier, who didn't know if Rembrandt were Dutch? Think for a moment if ye were he, or any one of these runners—used to being out and about on their own, roaming the city in their thief taking—locked up in here, night after night, guarding a lot of art work they can't afford, don't understand and don't care about. How would ye feel were that ye?"

"Irritable."

He kissed her nose as a reward for her insight. "At best. And we are going to take advantage of that circumstance, and make them even more irritable by setting off the alarm."

"But will they not know we have done so when the statue is gone?"

"But we shan't take the statue. Not yet. Not until we have made them irritable beyond caution."

"You mean to harass them into inaction? Good God, that is diabolically clever. What a scoundrel you are."

Upon her lips, it sounded like a compliment. "Thank ye." This time, he rewarded her by kissing her plum sweet lips. "I only hope it works according to plan. I have done my research on Mr. Tildesley's patent intrusion alarms, and the secret, I think, will be in setting it off, but in making it look like a malfunction. Wish me luck."

She tipped her head up, and shyly, slowly leaned in to offer him a soft kiss.

It was all the reward he could ever ask for. "I always knew I was the luckiest man in the world. All right then." He checked his watch one last time.

It was now or never.

"Stay here," he instructed, before he shuttered the glim, eased open the closet door, and cautiously tiptoed out into the empty exhibition space.

Empty, except for one very special, very well protected statue of Diana by Verrocchio.

Which he suspected was not truly a Verrocchio at all. But which he intended to steal anyway.

Chapter 18

EVEN THOUGH SHE was watching from the shelter of the closet door, and even though he had warned her, and even though she had warned herself, nothing could have prepared Mignon for the unholy din that was the sound of the Tildesley alarm lock going off.

It was as if a runner were actually taking a hammer to the bell, so loudly and incessantly did it ring. And as soon as he set if off, Rory came pelting back across the floor, and into the closet, and into her arms.

And even though Rory did flick the lock on the closet door before he pulled it shut, locking them in, she did not mind. Because this time, it felt safe and secure. Because the moment the door closed, he took her in his arms, kissing her passionately, before he urged her down to the floor, and into their low hiding place under the stair.

In comparison with the first time the runners had made their organized rounds of the exhibition rooms, this time was utter chaos—their footfalls were thunderous as they ran from one room to the next, shaking the very walls of the closet as they pounded up and down the stairs in their haste to check every single lock upon every single window and door.

There must have been a great many locks.

But they seemed to have located the alarm under the Diana statue, for the din finally ceased, and from their vantage point under the stair, they could hear a conversation close by.

"Everythin's in order, sir," a voice reported.

Another voice confirmed, "Nothin' is missin'."

"Damned alarm went off for no reason," another groused.

Mignon could feel Rory's unrestrained grin against her forehead. "Why are you smiling?" she asked in a whisper.

"Because it's working—they're getting annoyed."

Outside, in the exhibition space, more footfalls could be heard tramping back down the stair. "Are all the alarms reset?"

"Aye, gov'nor," and "Aye, sir," came the responses, but it was a longer while until all of the footsteps finally retreated, and silence once again reigned over the empty rooms.

Mignon's heart eased slowly back into a more normal rhythm. More normal, but not entirely normal—because she wasn't normally lying under a stair with a handsome man plastered all down the length of her with his legs tangled in her skirts. Because never before this evening had a man put his hand so intimately into the small of her back, and held her tight, and kissed her until she thought her heart would rise out of her body. Never before had she laid her head against a gentleman's chest and listened to the strong steady beat of his heart.

It was certainly a night for firsts.

Rory eased back and reached for the glim, and the low mellow light illuminated their hiding spot once more. "All right, then?"

"Almost. Even though I knew what would happen, my heart was thumping as if it would come right out of my chest."

"I'm sorry for the fright. Ye've been an absolute sport about this. I could not have asked for a better confederate in crime."

"It must be my tainted blood." Her papa was a scoundrel of the first order—why should she not be a scoundrel of some lesser order? Perhaps all her trying to be good and safe and normal was just working against her own true nature. Perhaps she was destined to become a lady thief. "But I do not know if I could stand the worry and the constant fright. I had no idea what you had to endure. If I had known I doubt I would have had the courage to ask you to you this."

"Well, that's very kind of ye to say. I do appreciate yer consideration. But if ye hadn't asked me, what would ye have done about Mr. Cathcart?" He said the name quietly, watching her face for her reaction.

Which was, she feared, all too obvious—she felt stupid and lightheaded, as if all the blood drained from her heart, leaving her hollow and empty. Even her voice was faint. "How do you know about Mr. Cathcart?"

"It's my business to know," he said in a perfect echo of what he had said that first night, when he had known her father would be out at the exhibition. He put his hands on her shoulders to steady her. "And I know that tomorrow, he is supposed to turn up to test your ten thousand guinea Verrocchio."

She tried to swallow, to ease the breath she couldn't seem to draw, but her throat was too tight, her mouth too dry.

But she didn't have to speak. He already knew—she could see the hard knowledge in his eyes, even though he spoke quietly to soften the blow. "It's a forgery, isn't it?"

There didn't seem to be any point in lying now, and he deserved to know, really, while he was putting his life and certainly his liberty on the line for her. But the admission of one forgery would no doubt lead to another, and she had to at least try and keep Papa out of it. "Well, you see…" she hedged.

"Nay." He stopped her with a firm squeeze on her shoulder. "We haven't got time for long involved stories at this time of night—and our business is not yet finished. So if ye please, just nod your head, aye or nay. Is the Diana a forgery?"

She closed her eyes against the shame of it, but she nodded.

"Ah," was all he said, but when she opened her eyes to look up at him, his face was suffused with a look of warm satisfaction. "I was right," he explained. "I thought there was something fishy right from the start. But it's too old, too well known in the Blois Collection, even before the revolution. And besides, yer father never studied sculpture that I know of."

And it was his business to know all about her Papa. Her gentleman thief had a wealth of knowledge she had never dreamed of.

"Who carved it?" he asked.

Mignon took a deep cleansing breath, and gave herself the relief of telling the truth for once. "My grandfather."

"Ah. The old *comte*'s brother, yer father's father? I see." He ran a hand into his bright, sandy hair, as if in contemplation. "And who posed for it?"

"My grandmother."

"Aah." This time, his smile was all pleased mischief, spreading across his face like jam. "I was right—there is a resemblance between ye and that statue." He kissed her on the tip of her nose, as if that would prove it.

"You are the only one who has ever noticed," she grumbled. But Mignon was glad it was out in the open—it felt as if a great weight had been lifted from her shoulders. But still, she wasn't altogether comfortable—they were still locked in a closet in Somerset House, and they still had to steal the statue to keep it from the diabolical Mr. Cathcart.

"Well, I'm very sensitive and perceptive about beauty." Rory tipped his head in that charming, considering way of his, and ran the backs of his fingers down her neck in a lovely, sweet caress that eased her discomfort.

"When did you suspect that the statue was a forgery?"

He smiled, and tipped his head to the other side, as if he might hedge. But then he said, "The moment ye asked me to steal it."

If he hadn't had his arms around her, Mignon thought she might have fallen down, so unexpected was his answer. "But if you knew...then...why? Why are you in a closet with me in Somerset House in the middle of the night, helping me to steal back a worthless forgery?"

"Because," he said solemnly, "I like ye." And then he kissed her.

He kissed her with something more than mere like. He kissed her with passion and heat, and something more elusive—something new, that she hadn't met with before.

He kissed her with promise.

A promise of trust and loyalty and abiding, steadfast warmth and safety.

He kissed her as if she mattered.

What a strange thought. She had always mattered to herself, and to Papa she supposed. But it was altogether different to matter to someone like Rory Andrews, a clever, dangerous thief. But a person she had come to hold in such regard.

"You love me," she said, as much to convince herself as him. "I think you must."

"I think I must." His next kiss was slower—it took him forever to lower his lips to hers, all the time staring down at her with that absolutely focused smile—but even more filled with carnal intent. He kissed her with hunger, as if he might devour her. As if only she could feed the hunger within him.

Until she could not.

Because he pulled abruptly back. "I almost forgot. Ye're engaged."

"Not at all, truly," she hastened to assure him. "I only got engaged to get rid of him. Because he would not take no for an answer. Even though it is the only answer I mean to give him."

His chest expanded with the breath he let out. "So ye're definitely not going to marry the Duke of Bridgewater?"

"Definitely not." How could she marry someone like the Duke of Bridgewater, when she was falling quite in love with another man?

"That's better, then. May I kiss the bride-not-to-be?"

She felt as if her smile might take wing and fly her into his arms. "Oh, yes please."

But she kissed him just as much as he kissed her. She was too full of something beyond hunger, beyond want. Something that filled her head with daydreams, and her heart with a longing that could only be called hope.

They were becoming dangerous, his kisses. They made her feel as if anything were possible. As if there might somehow be a future for her with a forger for a father, and a gentleman thief as something altogether more singular, and intimate.

He smoothed the hair away from her face, and then opened the shutters on the small lantern to check his watch. "Second lap around the course, coming up. Are ye ready?"

"For the alarm? If you can stand that din, then I must as well."

"Good sport. Don't go away." He rubbed his thumb along her bottom lip before he kissed her one last time. "I want to mark my place."

And then he slipped out into the darkness of the exhibition space, and once again set off the alarm under the Diana statue. He was back in a flash, taking the hand she held out to him, locking the door, and then folding himself into her as they slid into their hiding place in the cool dark under the stair.

Outside the cozy confines of their closet, chaos reigned, but not quite as energetically as before. Though they could hear footfalls tramping out into the rooms and up the stairs, this time the guards steps were not as rushed. In fact some were downright sluggish. Even when they came right to the closet door.

"Lot of rot, this is," the unseen guard muttered as he fumbled with the closet key, and opened the door just as the alarm was turned off.

Mignon tucked her head into Rory's chest, and squeezed herself into the smallest, stillest bundle possible, while the runner fumbled with something on one of the closet's small shelves—something liquid, that sloshed in its bottle, and had a cork that popped off with an audible squeak.

"Ahh," the runner breathed out his relief.

"D'ya hear tha?" Another set of footsteps drew near.

"What?"

Mignon—and she assumed Rory as well—could hear him shove his bottle back onto the shelf, where it tipped over.

"Yar man at the door. 'E sez as someone come from the Duke of Northumberland next door. Sent his man round to ask what all the damn racket wus."

"Did'ya tell the guvner?"

"I did. He dint like it, not one bit."

"I'll lay ya a groat 'e turns that bleedin' mal-functionin' thing off."

With that the runner slammed the closet door closed, and locked it. And then the alarm bell rang out one more time, before it was abruptly cut off.

Then the footsteps retreated. And silence reigned.

Under the stairs, Rory didn't move, presumably waiting and listening. But when nothing else happened—no sound, nothing but silence—he sighed, as if he had been holding his breath. "My God," he finally breathed. "I think it worked. I'll have to test it of course, but I think it actually worked. I think he actually has turned the blasted thing off."

Chapter 19

RORY'S VOICE WAS full of astonished wonder.

"Why are you so surprised?" she asked.

"Because...theory is all well and good, but one never knows, does one?" He began to scoot his way backwards, out from under the stair.

Mignon followed. "Of course one does, when one is a top notch gentleman thief."

"Ah, yes." His exhalation of relief carried a quiet chuckle. "What an extraordinary feeling." He opened up the shutter on the lantern and held out his hand to help her up. "Come. Let's go test our theory, and see if we can get our sham Verrocchio."

He made quick work of picking the lock one last time, and peered cautiously into the dark exhibition space. "Wait here, while I see if it worked. If not, prepare yourself for round three."

She nodded and put her hands up to cover her ears.

"Oh, wait." He turned back. "One more thing." He directed the thin beam of the glim toward the shelves, and found the runner's hidden bottle of gin. "This will do nicely."

Armed with the gin, Rory made his silent way across to

the statue, but this time, when he tipped the Diana off her pedestal, silence reigned.

Nothing happened. No alarm, no hue and cry. Nothing.

The alarm had been well and truly disabled—Mr. Tildesley's Patent alarm locks had been made patently useless.

"Perfect." Her gentleman thief cradled the Verrocchio in his arms like a baby, and replaced her with the gin bottle before he tip-toed back to Mignon. "Here's yer worthless, ten thousand guinea baby."

"Thank you. It is quite remarkable to have the troublesome thing back. What a lot of bother she has caused."

"Oh, I don't know." He took a critical look at the thing. "Yer grandpapa was pretty damn good, ye ken. To say nothing of grandmama." He carefully pulled the cleaning bucket with Mignon's discarded poplin gown out of the closet. "Wrap her up tight in those skirts. Carefully. And into the bucket she goes."

When they had arranged the statue to their liking in the bottom of the deep bucket, "Now what?" she asked.

"Now, yer job is, no matter what happens, stay down on yer knees and keep scrubbing, moving in the direction of that guard's room." He pointed across the exhibition hall toward the doorway through which all the runners had disappeared.

"But the guard's room will be full of runners."

He shook his head. "The moment the cry goes up that the Verrocchio is gone," he whispered, "there will be runners everywhere *but* the guard's room."

"Oh, yes. I see exactly."

"Clever lass. Now into the chimney piece with ye, until the charwomen get here and start to scrub. And don't stop until ye get to the guard's room. Don't let anyone, or anything stop ye."

"I will not let them stop me," she swore.

He smiled down at her. "Ye've a cobweb on yer dingy old cap. And dirt and dust all over yer skirts. And ye are still the most remarkably beautiful lass I have ever seen."

Mignon could feel her face heat with pleasure. Even though she was locked in a museum with a priceless, worthless statue they had just stolen, in the middle of the night, with a gentleman thief she was falling in love with, she didn't know when she had been happier.

But she was even happier the next moment, when he kissed her sweetly upon the corner of her mouth, and whispered, "Remarkable lass." And pushed her down into the chimney piece.

Which was a great deal roomier, but a great deal less comfortable without his presence.

And though it worried her that she had no idea where he had taken himself off to hide, she did not have long to wait. Just as the clock above the mantelpiece chimed out midnight, a unseen door could be heard opening, followed by the boisterous, businesslike voices of the charwomen, who filed past to retrieve mops and pails from the closet, and quickly set to work.

Mignon simply waited until they had worked their way close to her, and then she backed out of the empty fireplace as if she had been in there scrubbing all along.

She edged in behind two beefy-looking ladies who were having a good chatty coze.

"So I sez, 'Oo do you fink yer talkin' to, I sez, and then I sez, I knows me worf.'"

"You tell 'im, hen."

Mignon had a start when she heard the runners start to filter out into the exhibition space, until it became clear they were just there to chat and flirt with the char women, who were clearly happy to pause in their work.

"'Ello, 'ello, Doris, m'girl. Good night of it?"

"Yeah, all right. You?"

Mignon edged away, and pulled her dingy cap down around her face to stay inconspicuous.

"Had a right cropper 'ere," the runner answered.

Doris sat up, and put her hands to her copious hips. "Did'ja now? Heard there was a to-do."

"You don't know the 'alf of it," was the runner's answer. "Hasn't the bloody special alarm under that ruddy statue there"—he flung his arm in the direction of the statue.

And saw, along with the rest of them, a gin bottle instead.

"Oh, bloody everlastin' 'ell!" he exploded. "Alarm," he called at the top of his voice. "Alarm!"

Mignon had almost made it all the way to the doorway, and she didn't have to fake her own shriek of alarm when the runners came piling out of the guard's room. "'Ere!" she added for authenticity's sake.

But the moment after they all come storming by, shouting and yelling at each other, she scooted right in behind them, and shut the guard's room door. She would have turned the lock, but the door burst open behind her, she was being hauled up off her feet by one of the runners.

But before she could think, or scream, or kick him hard in the shins, he kissed her.

And she melted against him. "Rory."

"Shhh. Right this way. Quickly." He took the cleaning bucket out of her hand and led her out the back of the room, down a stair to the basement, and through a catacomb-like storage area, which must have once been the Somerset kitchens.

They came out into the night through a locked door that Rory picked open, on the lower level, on the opposite side of the house, close to the river. Rory led her along the embankment, following a path east until they arrived at an alley along the docks.

Where a well-remembered phaeton was waiting. With the same disreputable, lazy tiger. "All right then, guv'na?" He shoved himself to his feet.

"Absolutely, Archie. If ye'd take this." Rory handed over the bucket containing their precious cargo, and reached under the seat to produce a large great coat for himself and a long, black velvet cloak for her. "Put this on to cover those clothes. And let us be rid of that marvelously atrocious cap."

He pulled the nasty old thing off her head, disrupting her pins and making her hair tumble down over her shoulders. But she had no time to put it back up, as he was already settling the enveloping cloak across her shoulders and looping the clasp.

"Up ye go." He practically tossed her up onto the high perch seat. And then he was slinging his own coat on over the livery, taking the top hat the tiger, Archie, handed him, before he climbed up beside her. "Spring 'em."

And they were away, with the river and Somerset House rapidly lost from view as they rolled around the corner and headed north. He knew his way well, winding them through the Clare Market, and then west and north again, in a random pattern that finally brought them around the back of Soho Square to her house, where she would be safe and sound. Where all was right with the world.

Rory handed her down like a gallant, and if his hands perhaps lingered overlong at her waist, she did not mind. In fact, she welcomed it.

At least until she caught sight of nosy Mrs. Parkhurst twitching the curtains over to have a better peek from next door.

Rory noticed too. "She saw us, yer neighbor."

"She sees everything," Mignon sighed. Not that she had ever given the old woman something to see.

"Yer reputation, I'm afraid, will be in tatters," he teased.

"About time." Nothing could mar her good spirits tonight, not even the threat of Mrs. Parkhurst's wagging tongue. "I am sure my personal reputation can withstand this small blow, as long as my family's reputation stays intact. And if the old woman puts anything about, I shall say that your tiger was here to chaperone us."

"Ah, yes, Archie. He's the soul of discretion." Rory spoke over his shoulder at the young man. "Act discreet, as well as pious, Archie. Ye should be able to manage that."

Mignon laughed, and took the hand Rory offered to walk her to her steps.

"What are we to do with...her?" she asked in a low

voice, referring to the Diana. "I cannot take her within. Papa will…" She couldn't begin to explain what a scoundrel like her father might be tempted to do with a stolen and forged statue. Not to mention that their home might be the first place the Bow Street Runners might choose to search, should the robbery of the statue somehow point their way.

All her relief at getting the statue away from Somerset House dissolved into a new bundle of worries, lodging deep inner chest.

Her gentleman thief remained entirely unperturbed. "I think I may be able to help."

And just like that, she could breathe again. "That would be much appreciated. I suppose you can use your criminal connections and fence it along?"

"Miss Blois, ye astonish me." He was smiling at her in his roguish, teasing manner. "What do ye know of fences?"

"My grandfather and my father were, and are forgers, Rory. I suppose I know a lot of things I have never admitted to before. And tonight, I have done a lot of things I have never done before. An evening for firsts, all around."

"An evening for firsts, and lasts." He smiled down at her. But before she could ask exactly what 'lasts' might mean, he went on. "Ye may safely leave the statue to me."

"I will. It is only right that you have the Diana as some recompense for the theft—it is not as if we could ever display it again…"

"Of course. Consider it done."

And just like that, they were done. And she was done with excitement and daring-do. Because despite her brief foray as an amateur thief, she was still quiet little Mignon Blois who liked being home, safe and sound. Nothing could ever really change that.

Not even a handsome gentleman thief.

From whom she had to part—at least for now. "Thank you." She extended her hand to him. "For everything."

"Ye are most welcome. For everything." His smile was everything kind and wonderfully rueful. "I would kiss ye, but Archie's sensibilities are easily overset."

It was a good thing it was dark, so he couldn't see the blush sweeping across her face.

On second thought, she didn't care if he saw it—she wanted him to. She wanted him to know how she felt about him. And she could only hope that feeling was mutual.

"Good night, Rory Andrews."

His voice, soft and full of bittersweet pleasure, said it was. "Good night, my sweet Miss Blois."

Mignon stood on the steps, and watched her heart drive away, and hugged her accomplishment, along with her cloak, tight. It had been a marvelous night. And she hoped, and even more marvelous tomorrow. But she wouldn't know until then.

She would have let herself in with her key, safely stowed down her bodice, when the door was opened for her. "Mignon?"

It was her Papa, who stood on the doorstep staring at her. "Mignon, who was that man?"

"Papa do not tell me you have taken up snooping at the windows like old Mrs. Parkhurst?"

"Well, I could not help but notice that you seem to have been accompanied home by a tall, blue-eyed ruffian."

"Yes, yes, my ruffian." She urged Papa back inside and shut the door behind them, safe and sound. "Was he not marvelous?" She kissed her papa on both cheeks. "He has saved us, Papa. He has saved us all."

Papa's look was all narrow astonishment. "What do you mean?"

"Do you know what he has got hidden under the seat of that phaeton, Papa?"

Her father stilled, as if bracing for a blow. "No."

She smiled to show him it was all going to be all right—that there was no blow to come. They had already finessed the *coup de grace*. "He has got your Verrocchio, Papa."

Her father gasped, and clasped a hand to his chest.

Mignon guided her him to chaise. "He stole it for me, Papa. To save us." She patted his hand to assure him. "To keep the Verrocchio from that awful specialist Mr. Cathcart.

Is it not marvelous!"

Her papa began to regain a little of his color. "Stolen from Somerset House, this evening?"

"Yes. And I helped him. I was there, too." Even she could hear the pride in her voice.

"My darling angel," Papa breathed, and shook his head, as if he could not quite comprehend it. "It is astonishing. A marvel. Thank God for the criminal class."

"Yes." She could only agree. This evening the criminal class had been her guardian angel. "Is it not lovely? You do not have to go to gaol, and I do not have to go to the Americas. We can stay right here, where it is so, so much better."

"Enormously." Papa clapped his hand over his heart, and then shot to his feet. "Champagne, we must have champagne to celebrate." He looked at her, and clasped her hand again, and then kissed her on the forehead. "You really are the most remarkable daughter."

"Not nearly as remarkable as Mr. Andrews, my gentleman thief. He is the one who masterminded the whole affair. I just found him. That is all I did. Because I love you, Papa."

"My darling angel." Papa looked moved to tears. "I love you more." He wiped his eyes and shook his head, "Come, I will rouse Henri to find us some champagne, and we will celebrate your triumph."

"Our triumph. But just one glass, Papa. I really am terribly exhausted. And I have to get up early, and go to Brooks's."

"Brooks's," Papa echoed. "I am beginning to like the sound of this Brooks's."

Chapter 20

RORY ANDREWS CATHCART slept like a baby, clear of conscience and with a smile on his face, despite the fact that the lady with whom he slept was made out of cold marble. Because she was merely a placeholder for the real thing—the real woman he meant to claim this morning. As soon as he had some breakfast.

Not even the sight of two of his best friends eating all his kippers could put him off. "Gentlemen." He greeted them with all the *bonhomie* and goodwill he was feeling.

"Your triumph is all over the morning papers, Rory. Word must have got out quickly." Alasdair folded the *Times*, and read, "'Priceless Statue Stolen from Somerset House.' And 'Royal Academy Robbed.' Though I salute your ingenuity in pulling this off, I do wish you hadn't created quite such a sensation, and left me a problem restoring confidence in law and order."

"I had my reasons, which ye'll be glad of." But Rory was not about to be made responsible for all the county's problems, but he was loath to give his reasons without a full audience. "Where's Archie?"

It wasn't like his friend and erstwhile tiger to miss breakfast—or any meal that someone else was providing.

"Messenger came for him about an hour ago," Ewan replied. "Ran out the door still tying his cravat."

"But it sounds as if he is already come back." Alasdair pulled back the curtain from the breakfast room window. "And he appears to be in the most enormous monstrosity of a carriage. Good Lord—the things people would rather have than their own money," he muttered in judgement. "Best see what he's about."

"Not until I've have breakfast." Rory held fast. "Or at the very least a very hot cup of very strong coffee. Standards must be maintained even with Archie flying about the place like an unleashed circus monkey."

The unleashed circus monkey pounded through the front door, up the stairs, and flung his hat across the room with all the drama of a diva upon the stage at the Paris opera. "Do ye want to know who sent me home in that carriage?"

Rory took a long, fortifying sip of his coffee, and put his booted feet up on an empty chair. "A fellow never boasts of his conquests, Archie. It's not gentlemanly."

"No, it's not a lady, damn yer eyes. It's a man."

"Archie, please. We're at breakfast. And I repeat, a gentleman never boasts about his conquests, no matter what sort they are."

Archie colored past his hairline. "Damn yer eyes," he repeated. "Are ye going to let me tell?"

"You want to tell us." Alasdair joined in the ribbing. "But do we *want* to know?"

"Oh, aye." Archie nodded vigorously. "I rather think ye *do* want to know."

"Then from *whom* did ye accept a ride in that carriage, Archie?" Rory asked. Just because he was a gentleman thief entertaining a gallery of rogues at his breakfast was no reason to abandon good grammar.

Archie presented his information like a gift. "Bridgewater."

"The Duke thereof? Rabid collector?" And potential future husband of his very own Mademoiselle Mignon du Blois.

The thought brought Rory up short. Damn it, while basking in the heat of their triumph last night, he hadn't quite got around to making sure that the Duke of Bridgewater *never* had a chance to become Mignon Blois's husband. Because she was going to marry him, and become Mrs. Rory Cathcart.

Just as soon as he told her who he was.

"Indeed," Archie was rubbing his hands together. "And do ye want to know what the Duke of Bridgewater was asking me if I know anything about?"

Well, good goddamn. Could Mignon have said anything to Bridgewater this morning, perhaps breaking off their engagement? But it was not as if he, Rory Andrews, had given her a reason—besides kissing her senseless—to officially break off her engagement. They had not discussed the future. They had exchanged no understandings.

But what else could Archie be talking about, unless... "The Verrocchio?"

"The Verrocchio," Archie confirmed. "Aye. And do ye want to guess why?" Archie was enjoying himself.

Rory was not sure if he was. "He wants to impress Miss Blois, and avenge her loss?"

"Miss Blois?" Archie's face went blank. "No, not a chance of it. He wants to buy it."

"He wants to buy the Verrocchio?" Rory shot to his feet. "He wants to buy stolen property?"

"Yes. Exactly. Turns out the Duke of Bridgewater has some rather athletically bendable scruples."

"My God." Now that he was standing, Rory found he had to move. He paced toward the door, forcing Alasdair to move his feet.

"Careful."

Rory didn't care if he trod all over Alasdair's rather large, expensively shod feet—he had other, more important fish to fry. But he had to hook the damn great big fish first. And keep himself, and his friends, entirely in the clear. "Why did he come to ye?"

Archie smiled. "I'm only an intermediary. Like ye, I've

acquired a certain reputation for knowing things that generally don't want to be known, but it's ye Bridgewater thinks has a finger on the pulse of the art world."

"What did ye tell him?"

"That I would make inquiries, and we would see what we could see."

"Excellent." So far, so good. But what came next? Could he work it so that the forged statue never saw the light of day, but kept the Blois family from any hint of wrong-doing?

It could work. They would make it work. "He understands that he will have a work of art that he can never speak of, never acknowledge, never display even in his own house, ever?"

"Absolutely," Archie confirmed. "He wants it only for his own personal satisfaction and pleasure, he said. Just to know it was his, that he had stolen a march on his rivals, would be enough."

"Well then." Rory smoothed down his waistcoat. "I think we should sell it to him."

Archie slid a smile across his face. "Aye. For an enormous fee."

Something that must have been his own rather exercised scruples reared up in objection. "No. That would be wrong Archie." For many reasons, but mostly just one. "Because it's not a Verrocchio. It is a forgery."

Archie's mouth hung open in utter astonishment "Ye don't say."

"I do say. I had my suspicions, but she admitted it to me last night, confessed in the heat of battle, as it were. Made years ago, before the current count was even born." That was stretching the truth a little, but protecting the current Comte du Blois was important to him now.

At that news, even Alasdair came to his feet. "So our instincts were right all along." he gazed at Rory thoughtfully. "What are you going to do?"

Rory took a good deep breath, and let it out slowly. "I'm going to let ye dispose of the Verrocchio to the Duke of

Bridgewater, in good time and with certain conditions—the most important and inviolable of which is that he must break off all contact with the Blois family, and with Miss Mignon Blois in particular."

"All right." Archie looked at the others for their agreement, and when he got it, he turned back to Rory. "And then what?"

"And then I think I'm going to go out and get myself engaged."

Archie let out a slow whistle. "Ye don't say."

Rory was sure. He had never been so sure in all his life. "I do."

Chapter 21

MIGNON DRESSED CAREFULLY, in her finest day dress of embroidered lemon silk and white lace. For the first time in what felt like ages, she wanted to look her absolute best. Just in case. Just in case her gentleman thief should come to steal something else.

But the person who came was not the gentleman thief, but the gentleman who had been robbed—Sir Joshua Reynolds.

Henri's announcement of their visitor only just gave Papa time to rearrange his visage into appropriately mournful lines. "My dear sir, what has happened?" He gestured to the morning papers with open astonishment. "How could this be?"

"My dear sir, I am everything apologetic. I can't begin to understand how it could have happened—it was there one moment and gone the next."

"The audacity!" Papa railed. "To wake to such news—" He clasped a dramatic hand to his heart. "It pains me so."

Mignon did her best to look stern to quash any further theatrics, and asked instead. "What can you tell us, Sir Joshua?"

"Only that the Diana is gone, snatched in the most

audacious manner from under the noses of the Bow Street Runners hired specifically to guard it. We are beyond understanding how."

Papa allowed himself to sink into a chair with his hand to his brow, as if in mortal pain. But he still had enough of the scoundrel to ask, "But insurance cover was taken with Lloyd's, so we will be recompensed for the loss of the statue—though it was entirely priceless, one of a kind?"

Here Sir Joshua looked more than pained—his face was pale and pasty with upset. "I regret that the cover had not yet taken effect, Count Blois, as the technical examination with the expert from Christie's was still pending."

This time, Papa did not have to playact his astonishment—he clutched his chest at the pain of the blow. "No."

"Unfortunately, yes." Sir Joshua took out an immaculate handkerchief to mop his brow. "I am afraid that there will be no recompense for the loss."

Papa sat in utter, stunned silence. Whether it was acting or not, Mignon would not tell.

There was nothing for her to do but show poor Sir Joshua out. And then prepare to give Papa the rest of the bad news—that even if she had been the one to steal it, the Verrocchio was not coming back.

"Another gentleman to see you, *Mademoiselle*," Henri called to her retreating back as she went up the stairs. "A Mr. Andrews of Brooks's Club, though he does not appear to have a card."

Mignon dismissed Rory's lack of social standing with a gesture meant to hurry Henri along. "Show him in, show him in. To the salon."

While Henri did so, Mignon hastened to arrange herself on the divan in the salon, attempting to appear all that was cool and composed, when she was practically bouncing on her seat.

But in another moment, there he was, her gentleman thief, standing in her salon impeccably dressed, hat and gloves in hand, smiling at her in best the fairy tale fashion.

"Rory" She stood and held her hand out to him, willing herself not to be nervous. Willing everything to be all right.

"Miss Blois." Her gentleman thief came to her straightway, taking her hand to kiss. "Thank ye for seeing me."

She ignored his formality, and the hint of something dire and unpleasant in his voice. "As if I would not see you." She led him to the sofa to sit next to her. "I have been hoping all morning that you would call. And you have. And I cannot seem to stop smiling. I must look like a lunatic, but I am so happy. And I owe it all to you."

"Miss Blois," he glanced at Henri, who was reluctantly excusing himself out the doors, "Ye're too kind."

His voice was growing more distant, but she wouldn't allow it. She wouldn't. "I am not being kind, I am being factual. You have saved us. You must know that. You must."

"I'm honored to have helped. But before ye say anything else, there is something I must tell ye."

Mignon braced herself for bad news even as she refused to hear it. "It is quite all right. You need not tell me anything, really. You owe me nothing, although I hope this job has seen you into good money. I should be curious to know what you make from the sale of the Verrocchio, or what you hope to make—purely professional curiosity, you know."

"There is no profit to make." He shook his head even as he smiled. "Because that would be dishonest."

Mignon went still, holding her breath so she might be sure she had heard him aright. "What do you mean?"

"I mean I'm not a thief. At least not a professional, full-time thief." He took her hands and looked into her eyes while he spoke, as if he was making sure she heard and understood him.

Which she did not. "Are you not? Then what were you doing in our house? Taking the Hals…" That chilly feeling seeping into her chest was reality, rearing its ugly, insistent head.

"I am a specialist in fraudulent art," her gentleman non-thief explained even as he held her hand and inched closer. So close their foreheads were nearly touching. "I am an expert in detecting, finding and exposing forgeries and all manner of falsities in the provenance of art. And I have been laboring under an alias, or a sort of truncated version of the truth. Because my name—my real name—is Rory Andrew Cathcart."

"Cathcart? You are Mr. Cathcart?" It was as if the floor had moved beneath her feet—Mignon felt she might have fallen over if he had not continued to hold her hand tight.

"The same." He nodded slowly, never taking his eyes from her face.

"You are not a gentleman thief."

"No. Though, I hope I can call myself a gentleman."

"But what were you doing here? That night you broke in—" Mignon looked over at the wall where the *Cavalier* laughed down at her.

"I was trying to have a look at yer Hals, which I suspect yer brilliant papa painted, when ye loomed up like an avenging ghost in yer white night clothes, and conked me over the head with yer pike."

"It was a halberd." Mignon didn't know what else to say—there was nothing else she could say. Everything she thought was false—a forgery.

He was nothing that she had thought him to be.

But he was still sitting next to her, holding her hand as if he did not want to let go, and she could not understand why—

"Good afternoon."

Mignon practically jumped out of her seat, astonished to find her father in the doorway of the salon. "Oh, Papa." Her heart was ringing a peal in her chest. "You surprised me."

"Mignon, I do not believe I have met your friend." Papa came forward with his hand extended. "Charles Blois. How do you do."

"*Monsieur le Comte.*" Her erstwhile gentleman thief bowed elegantly. "Rory Cathcart."

"Ah, the Honorable Mr. Cathcart. Of the ruthless, tall blue eyes."

"I beg yer pardon?"

Mignon had nothing but manners to fall back upon. "Papa, this is a friend of mine. He is—

"Yes, yes, Mr. Cathcart. Quite good looking, though a terrible man. No sense of guilt or shame." Papa sat himself comfortably in a chair. "I believe we have some interests in common, young man."

Mignon gaped as Mr. Cathcart—how could she call him Rory when she did not seem to know the slightest thing about him anymore?—and her papa put their heads together like two old friends. Two old, unscrupulous friends.

"We do, sir." Rory leaned forward. "Ye have two rather remarkable lasses in yer family, *Comte.*"

Papa nodded in clear agreement. "But the question is, which one do you intend to keep?"

"The real one."

"Ah." Papa's smile was slow, but spreading. "Very good choice, if I may say so."

Mr. Cathcart nodded in complete agreement. "I think so, too."

"And the other?" Papa did not even try to contain his enthusiastic curiosity.

"I have plans for her, too, Papa," Mr. Cathcart said. "I think ye'll approve. I've sold her to the Duke of Bridgewater."

"Aha!" Papa clapped his hands. "Perfection. He's the sort of man who would never think to have it verified. I've sold him several… Well, as you say, a very satisfactory conclusion. And what did you say he was going to pay, my son?"

"I didn't say, Papa." Mr. Cathcart smiled in his charming, mischievous way.

Papa was all smiling contentment as well—he leaned back in his chair as if he had eaten a fine, filling meal. "I hope you picked a nice round figure."

"I did." Mr. Cathcart—although it seemed even more

bizarre to call him Mr. Cathcart than Rory while he was calling her father 'Papa,' and Papa was calling him 'my son'—circumscribed the air with a figure. "Zero."

Papa lurched to his feet. "What?"

"Please be seated, *Monsieur le Comte*." Rory Andrews Cathcart, stood, and loomed over her papa, much the way he had loomed over her that first night. "Ye happen to be a forger. And I happen to be a man whose job it is to catch forgers, and put them in gaol."

For the first time in Mignon's memory, Papa began to look acutely uncomfortable. "Yes." He adjusted his cravat, as if it were suddenly too tight. "That seems to be problematic."

Rory nodded in agreement. "One of us is going to have to retire."

Papa considered this proposal for a short moment. "How do you propose we decide?"

"I tossed a coin on it."

"Ah?" Papa began to regain some color—the scoundrel in him no doubt plotting how he might turn either outcome to his advantage.

Rory was having none of that. "And ye lost," he added before her wily old father could deploy any of his wayward plans.

"But—" Papa sputtered. "How can that—"

"Come, Papa." Rory patted him on the back. "It's for the best. Ye had a great run. Ye're the best and ye know it—and so do I, and I had a pretty good look at that Hals. So why not hang up yer brushes, and go out while ye're on top. Never defeated, never caught, with paintings in half of the serious collections in London, and in *all* of the better collections in Norfolk, excluding my father's. But yer time at the easel is at an end," he declared. "So ye can either see out yer days here, and in the lovely home I'm going to make for yer daughter in the highlands, where ye can watch yer grandchildren grow, or we can go at it."

Happiness lit a cheery hearth fire within her, warming her from the top of her head to her toes. Making her believe, if only for the moment, that she could never be cold, or afraid of the dark again.

"Who knows," Rory went on. "Maybe one of yer grandsons will take after us both, and take up art."

At this news Papa brightened. "I never thought—" he mused. "Such a brilliant prospect."

Rory put his arm around Mignon, and asked her father, "What do ye say?"

The question was not just about Papa's future—it was about hers.

Papa thought for only a moment. "Here is my answer."

Papa took Rory's outstretched hand.

"Papa!" Hot salty tears were stinging Mignon's eyes, but she didn't care. She didn't care if her nose got red and her face got splotchy. Because she had never wept such tears of joy.

Papa embraced her, kissing her on the forehead. "Mignon my darling, for you, and for my grandchildren, I will give it up." He clasped his hand to his heart, but then drew suddenly back, all wide-eyed fright. "Tell me you have not already created my grandchild."

"Papa." Mignon could feel her face turn hot and pink. "No. My goodness, we're not even married."

"But, we will be posthaste," Rory clarified. "Once ye say the word."

"My children." Papa's face was wreathed in joy. "I give you my blessing."

"Thank you, Papa." She kissed her father on both cheeks, before Rory spoke.

"If ye will excuse us, Papa." Rory bowed very correctly to her father. "I beg a moment alone with yer lovely daughter."

"Of course, of course." Papa waved his arm in permission as he left them to their own devices. "I must order champagne, so we might all celebrate. Henri!" he called as he went. "Henri…"

And then she was alone with her gentleman.

Who promptly went down on one knee.

"My dearest Mignon." He took her hand, and for the first time in their association, her gentleman looked less than sure of himself. As if, for the first time, he might actually be afraid. "Before I can ask ye to make me the happiest of men, I must tell ye that I am not really a gentleman. I am a by-blow, the bastard youngest son of an earl, though he educated me, and gave me his name."

She did not care for names or titles—they had only ever brought her family trouble. She only cared for him. "You are a gentleman, in every action and in every word. Even if you are a bit of a scoundrel. But you must know that I come from a long line of utter and complete scoundrels, so you will be quite at home."

"I like yer scoundrels. And I like ye. I love ye."

"And I love you, too. If for no other reason than because in fifteen minutes you have convinced my Papa to do what I could not in fifteen years of pleading, and put down his brushes."

"Will ye only marry me for yer papa?"

"No." She didn't know how it was possible to cry and still be so happy, all at the same time. "I will marry you solely for myself. Because I am mad about you, my would-be gentleman thief. Mad for your love."

Please turn the page for an exciting excerpt from
Elizabeth Essex's first Highland Brides novel

MAD ABOUT THE MARQUESS

Available Now!

Edinburgh, Scotland
June 1792

LADY QUINCE WINTHROP had always known she was the unfortunate sort of lass who could resist everything but temptation. And the man across the ballroom was temptation in a red velvet coat. There was something about him—some aura of English arrogance, some presumption of privilege—that tempted her beyond reason, beyond caution, and beyond sense. Something that tempted her to steal from him. Right there in the Countess of Inverness's ballroom. In the middle of the ball.

Which was entirely out of character. Not the stealing—she stole as naturally as she breathed. But because the other thing that Lady Quince Winthrop had always known, was that the most important thing about stealing was not *where* one relieved a person of his valuable chattels. Nor *when*. Nor *how*. Nor even *what* particular wee trinket one slipped into one's hidden pockets. Nay.

The tricky bit was always *from whom* one stole.

When one robbed from the rich, one had to be careful. Pick the wrong man, or woman for that matter—too canny, too important, too powerful—and even the perfect plan could collapse as completely as a plum custard in a cupboard. Which made it all the more curious when she ignored her own advice, and picked the wrong man anyway.

Whoever he was, he stood with his back to her, his white-powdered hair in perfect contrast to that red velvet coat so vivid and plush and enticing that Quince was drawn to it like a Spanish bull to a bright swirling cape. Unlike the gaudily embroidered suits worn by the other men, the crimson coat was entirely unadorned but for two gleaming silver buttons that winked at her in the candlelight, practically begging her to nip one of the expensive little embellishments right off his back.

A button like that could feed a family of six for a fortnight.

And while her itchy-fingered tendency toward theft was perhaps not the most sterling of characteristics in an otherwise well brought up young Scotswoman, no one was perfect. And it was so very hard to be *good* all the time.

She had much rather be bad, and be *right*.

So Quince took advantage of the terrific crush in Lady Inverness's ballroom, slipped her finger into the tiny ring knife she kept secreted in the muslin folds of her bodice for just such an occasion, and sidled up behind Crimson Velvet.

She did not pause, nor give herself a moment to think on what she was about to do. She ignored the chitter of warning racing across her skin, and set straight to it, diverting his attention by brushing her bodice quite purposefully against his back, while she nipped the button off as easily as if it were a snap pea in a garden.

The elation was like a rush of blood to the head— intoxicating and addictive.

And because that was what she did—regularly stole fine things from finer people in the finest of ballrooms—she wasn't satisfied with only the one button. Nay. Another six mouths could be fed, and Quince could live all week on the illicit thrill of having taken the second button as well, and gotten away clean.

Except that she didn't get away clean.

She didn't get away at all.

A very large hand clamped onto Quince's wrist like a shackle. A red velvet-clad hand.

Alarm jumped onto her chest like a sharp-clawed cat, but Quince kept her head, automatically tucking the buttons and knife down the front of her bodice, and winding her now-empty free hand around that crimson velvet waist. She pressed herself to his backside more firmly, and familiarly, and said the first unexpected thing that came to her mind. "Darling!"

Crimson Velvet went as stiff as a bottle of Scotch whisky. "Good Lord. What's this?"

Alarm faded as recognition, and something that really oughtn't be delight curled into her veins. She knew that deceptively easy tone. Strathcairn. Earl thereof.

Oh, holy clotted cream.

The Laughing Highlander, she had once called him. But the Highlander was not laughing now. He was looking down at her with a sort of astonished wonder. "Wee Quince Winthrop, is that you? Good Lord." He stepped away—though he did not let go of her wrist—to case her as thoroughly as she ought to have done him. "I would not have recognized you."

She had clearly not recognized him. But the man gripping her wrist was neither the powdered dandy she had imagined from across the ballroom, nor the amusing, carefree Earl of Strathcairn she remembered. This man was different, and as dazzling in his own way as the shining silver buttons she had secreted down her soft-pleated bodice.

Firstly, he was as irresistibly attractive as that red velvet suit—all precise, well-cut shoulders, and long lean torso that seemed a far cry from the rangy, not-yet-fully-formed man in his youth. But secondly—and more importantly—he was much more controlled, more…curated, as if he had carefully chosen this particularly splendid view of himself to show the world. As if he not only wanted, but demanded to be *seen*.

Quite the opposite of Quince, who minded her appearance only to make sure she blended into the crowd—if her sister told her this season everyone was wearing white chemise dresses, then a white chemise dress she wore, disappearing into a sea of similarly dressed swans.

By contrast, Strathcairn looked every bit an individual, and quite, quite splendid. His waistcoat was of the same saturated color as his coat, and his snow-bright linen with only the barest hint of lace was the perfect foil for his immaculately powdered hair.

On any other man such a look might have appeared plain and underdone, but on Strathcairn the blaze of unadorned velvet served to highlight the force of his personality.

And there was nothing she liked as much as personality,

unless it was a challenge.

The earl appeared to be both.

"Why, Strathcairn." She made her voice everything breezy and cordial. As if her heart were not beating in her ears, and dangerous delight were not dancing down her veins. "It's been an age."

"Too long, from the looks of it." He stepped close—too close, not that she particularly minded—and looked down at her in a perilously attentive way, like a great, green-eyed tomcat eyeing up a wee mouse. The effect was most unsettling. It put her right off her stride. "Do you often embrace men you haven't seen in years?"

It had been exactly five years. He had briefly been one of her eldest sister Linnea's suitors then—newly elected a Member of Parliament, and headed to London, brilliant and ambitious. Quince remembered thinking the lanky Highlander was too tall, too clever, too canny, and far too insightful for tiny, fluttery Linnea, who adored nothing more than to be made a pet of.

Strathcairn hadn't seemed the type to keep pets.

Quince had been little more than a fourteen-year-old lass, but she had quite liked the young man's intelligence, nearly as much as his vibrant charm. Though what she liked best of all was his lovely, buttery smile that had made her feel like she was melting in the sun.

Strathcairn was certainly not pouring the butter boat over her now—his eyes might have been smiling, but from this angle, his chiseled jaw seemed to have been carved out of Grampian granite.

No matter. Quince was not Linnea—she was no one's pet. "I thought you were someone else," she lied without effort or qualm. "You've changed."

"So, my indiscreet young friend, have you." The barest hint of amusement in his glorious baritone was all that was necessary to bring back all the delicious torment of her youthful infatuation. "What in heaven's name did you think you were doing, calling me 'darling'?"

"Thought you were my Davie." Quince made up a

convenient beau on the spot. "I must find where the darling lad's got to."

Strathcairn let out a low, disbelieving bark of laughter, but didn't let go of her wrist. "You can't be old enough to be making assignations with men, wee Quince."

He trespassed easily on the old acquaintance by calling her by her Christian name—if Papa's botanically inspired names for his daughters could even be called Christian. Strathcairn also crossed the lines of familiar behavior by turning her toward the door, and somehow settling her against his side in such a subtle, but insistent, way, that not a person in the place would have suspected she was being all but frog-marched from the ballroom.

Even though she was grown up now, and towered over tiny Linnea, Quince still had to leg it to keep up with Strathcairn's long strides, all the while craning her neck to get a proper close look at him.

He looked so different, with his hair powdered white, and this controlled look upon his face, as if his smile had been put away in a cupboard, like a cravat that no longer fit. This new Strathcairn was far more imposing, and much, much more intimidating looming beside her like one of the great statues at Holyrood Palace than he had ever seemed all those years ago when she had keeked out at him from behind the drawing room curtains.

But she was not four and ten now. Quince let him tow her only as far as a conveniently empty alcove at the end of the entrance hall, before she rounded her elbow out of his grip, and served him a sharp, instructive jab in the ribs—anger brought out the Scots in her. "I'd be much obliged if you'd take your great paws off of me, Strathcairn. You're creasing my gown."

He subdued his grunt of discomfort, but put a hand absently to his side. "My *paws*"—he gave the word a wry intonation—"are not great in the least. They're rather average. For a Scot." At last he let the gorgeously rough Scots burr rumble beneath the town polish of his Member-of-Parliament accent. "Your gown is barely creased, and not by me, but by that interminable crush. Or more likely by this Davie fellow. And who the devil is he?" Strathcairn's green gaze poured over her like chilly water. "He can't possibly be a worthy mon if he lets a lass like you caress him in public. You're too young for suitors."

By jimble, but he had grown into an even more attractive man himself over the years, despite this polished, urbane facade. Or perhaps because of it—his worldliness gave him an attractive look of experienced wisdom. Quite irresistible.

"I'm not young anymore, either. I'm nineteen."

This he acknowledged with a wry sideways slant of his head, as if she were so out of kilter that the acute angle somehow made it easier to see her. "A very bad age to be an accomplished liar. And flirt." Strathcairn finally released her arm.

Much to her chagrin—which was all the emotion she would allow to account for the strange warmth suffusing her face—she found she missed the contact. How disconcerting.

So she changed the subject. Without flirting. "What are you doing in Edinburgh?"

"I've come north to see to Castle Cairn now that my grandfather's passed on."

Something that must have been sincerity stabbed her hard in the chest. "I am sorry, Strathcairn. He was a grand auld gent."

It was the right thing to say—Strathcairn's whole demeanor softened enough to show her more of the young man she had admired beneath his curated veneer. Even those glittering eyes went soft at the edges. "Thank you. He was, wasn't he?"

"Aye." The Marquess of Cairn had been a cavalier of the old school, gentlemanly, generous and bold. He had raised Strathcairn when his son, Strathcairn's father and the prior earl, had passed away suddenly during Straithcairn's youth. "He'll be missed. Oh—that means you're Cairn now."

Strathcairn—for she could think of him no other way even if he were now Marquess of Cairn—lowered that chiseled chin, and nodded in rueful agreement. "Aye. And he's left large boots to fill. So I'm seeing to Cairn." He took a deep breath as if he were collecting himself before he raised his head, and added, "But before I head north to home, I've also been asked to see to a rather persistent problem plaguing Edinburgh."

A softer sense of alarm—or perhaps it was guilt—padded across her shoulders like a stealthy barn cat. She made light of it, as she always did. "The persistent plague of too many ladies and not enough gentlemen? I do hope you've come prepared to dance."

The first hint of a smile began at the far corner of his lips, as if he were not yet ready to commit to the strenuous exercise of a full-out grin. "No. I rarely dance." He shook his head in rueful apology. "No, the problem I speak of is a rash of thefts from some of the better households in the district. I've been asked to restore some sense of law and order within Edinburgh's society."

"On guard" was too simple and sensible a phrase to describe her reaction—Quince's skin went a little cold, and that sharp-clawed sense of alarm scratched its way down her spine. But she rose to the occasion—she knew better than most how to put up her weapons. To win any sort of fight, one had to attack, not just defend. And satire was the sharpest sword of them all.

"*Restore* law and order?" She made herself suitably wide-eyed and breathless. "I hadn't realized we were lacking it. Ought we to be on watch for gangs of housebreakers?"

"No, no. Nothing like that." He looked sage and worldly with all his unruffled calm, but she could see a tinge of riddy heat creeping over his collar. "Though it's too early to tell. But certainly too early for worry. Pray don't be alarmed, lass."

Quince's skin went all over prickly—nothing put her back up like being condescended to.

She sharpened up her sarcasm so he would not be able to so easily evade her point. "Holy sticky toffee pudding, Strathcairn"—she decided if he could trespass upon her

Christian name, then she would trespass upon his old title—
"imagine that. A gang of cutthroat housebreakers carting off
priceless *Louis Quatorze* commodes to furnish their tatty
tenement houses. How have the newspapers and
broadsheets not been full of that?"

His smile confined itself to the outer corners of those
intelligent green eyes. "No priceless commodes have been
carted off."

"Auld occasional tables, then? Scaffy, mismatched
chairs?"

"You needn't mock, lass. It's not ladylike." He put a
hand up to rub the back of his neck, as if she really were
succeeding in making him uncomfortable. Marvelous. And
he had to subdue his growing smile—it started to hitch up
one side of his mouth, as if he wanted to be amused, but
was sure he oughtn't be. "If you must know, it's been very
small items—smelling salt bottles, buttons, and the like."

And her with his two buttons down her bodice. She
could feel them press into her skin as if they were biting her.
Unsurprising since they were *his*.

Quince was too larky a lass to let a bit of her discomfort
show. "Really? You've never abandoned Westminster, and
come all the way north from London for some missing
smelling salts?"

He had the good nature to look chagrined—that wary
smile turned down sheepishly at the corners. "Not exactly.
It's more complicated than that."

In fact, it was a great deal simpler than that. And she
could not resist telling him so. "Well, it's a very good thing
you told *me*." She lowered her voice in mock confidence.
"Because I'm sure I know exactly what's happened to
them."

He did not lean down to share her confidences. If
anything, he became more upright, and even tilted away
from her, as if he thought he could see her better from a
distance. "You, lass?"

"Aye." She seized him by the upper arms, and man-
handled him around—and by jimble if he hadn't the

brawest, most firmly shaped musculature hidden under that soft, plush velvet—so he could follow the direction of her gaze. "There. Mr. Fergus McElmore has misplaced his snuffbox there, right under that vase of heather and broom. See? And there"—she pushed him in the other direction— "the Dowager Countess of Chester has abandoned her silver vinaigrette bottle in the cushion of her seat. Q.E.D. as you parliamentary types say." She made a dramatic flourish as if she were a theatrical barrister in court. "There is the *modus operandi* of your thefts, Strathcairn—silly stupidity at worst, simple thoughtlessness at best. Though in Fergus' case particularly, I think the thoughtlessness has come from an excess of Lady Inverness's fine Scotch whisky befuddling his poor wee numptie brain."

A fine coloring heat crept up Strathcairn's neck to his jawline. It lessened that impression of Grampian granite nicely.

He shook his head, but smiled nonetheless. "You think me foolish."

"I think whoever complained of their missing baubles is foolish, when they are likely only victims of their own excess—how *can* they be expected to keep track of so many possessions?"

He looked at her then—really looked, as if he finally saw more of her than the ghost of her pigtailed past. "You've a remarkably jaundiced view of society for a lass your age."

She was more than jaundiced. She was nearly lock-jawed with disdain. "I have a realistic understanding of human nature, Strathcairn. I think people are forgetful, and don't want to appear foolish, so they bluster and blame others for their own mistakes. And it is easy enough to blame the powerless"—she nodded toward the servants, who were most often the first to be accused when anything went amiss—"from the safe position of privilege."

"I take your meaning, lass." He acknowledged the right of her argument with a nod. "Nevertheless, it is my duty to look into the matter, to determine if it is indeed only a case—or cases—of forgetfulness."

"Then I should advise you to start with our hostess, and ask her what she does with all the flotsam and jetsam her guests leave behind after her balls." Because not even Quince, terrible magpie that she was, could take everything that was available—her bodice could only hold so much. "Perhaps she has the footmen cart it all up, and take it to the poor box at Canongate Kirk where they'll get better use of it."

The moment the words were out of her mouth she wished them back. She'd let her tongue run away from her mind, and run far too close to the truth for comfort.

And her suggestion brought Strathcairn's perilously attentive green gaze back to her. "What an agile mind you have, Lady Quince." And then for no reason she could fathom, he smiled at her—that gorgeous, gleaming grin she remembered of old. That mischievous, sideways curve of lip that made her feel as if she were being blessedly bludgeoned over the head with a five-penny slab of butter.

Quince nearly had to pinch herself to call her wits back under starter's orders. "Oh, pish tosh. Practical is what my mind is."

His smile settled back down to the corner of those sharp eyes. "Perhaps, but you've given me an idea—perhaps what I'm looking for is not a hardened criminal, but someone with the dowagers's vice."

Nay, nay, nay.

Clever, too clear-eyed man.

She had to divert him with something equally clever. "Carrying a vinaigrette is a vice? What do you imagine the ladies keep in there? Undiluted opium?"

Strathcairn shook his head, but he was amused enough to still smile. "The dowager's vice is the irresistible tendency toward theft. That is, the compulsive stealing of objects which are not rightfully theirs. It is commonly practiced by maiden aunts and elderly companions. And dowagers, of course. Hence the name."

Oh, by jimble. That sounded far too apt.

And the skeptical Scot in him had taken over—he was

frowning at the row of seats at the far side of the ballroom where the older ladies, including some rather impecunious relations and companions, sat with their heads together in a comfortable coze. "They look perfectly harmless, but one never knows what might be hidden in their reticules, or tucked into their bodices."

Heat blossomed in that very place where Strathcairn's purloined buttons dug into her skin. Oh, he was clever.

But so was she. "Down their bodices?" She quite purposefully, and quite inexpertly, straightened her trim bodice, drawing his attention out the side of his eye to her small, but nevertheless eminently serviceable breasts. Mama always said a man couldn't think and look at breasts, no matter their size. No fool, Mama. And the clever padding Mama had insisted her maid sew into her stays made up for any natural deficit. "How do they find any room? Must be dreadful uncomfortable."

His brow rose as slowly as a guillotine over that acute eye. But his self-control was not equal to the task at hand, and his gaze strayed exactly where she had meant it to.

"Lady Quince." Strathcairn's lowered voice was absolutely irresistible when he forgot himself enough to let the Scots burr rumble. "Let me make right sure I understand you—are you *flirting* with me?"

"Am I?" Quince ignored the blaze of heat his voice and gaze kindled under her skin, and gave him her bright, knowing smile—all pleased lips and mischievous eyes. "What I am doing is trying to make you remember your duty, and accede to my wish to dance with me."

He regarded her with those too canny, too bright green eyes for another long moment before he answered. "Perhaps I will." He reached for her hand, and held her at arm's length for a lengthy perusal, as if he had not yet decided to grant her wish. "Yes, I definitely will. But before I do so, perhaps I ought to warn you, wee Quince, to be good. And be very, very careful what you wish for."

The heat that had blossomed under her bodice spread like wildflowers across her skin along the whole length of his gaze. And she liked it.

She raised her chin and gave him her slyest smile yet. "Oh, I am always careful, Strathcairn. But I had much rather be bad, and be *right*."

Please turn the page for an exciting excerpt from
Elizabeth Essex's next Highland Brides novel

*MAD, BAD, AND
DANGEROUS TO MARRY*

Coming Soon!

Castle Crieff, Scottish Highlands
1792

IT WAS ALWAYS going to be a delicate, tricky thing, to marry a man one had never met before one's wedding day. But until the moment the carriage rolled into the forecourt of Crieff Castle, Lady Greer Douglas had not suffered a single twinge of worry. For all that she had never met her bridegroom in person, she and the Duke of Crieff knew each other well.

Well enough to marry, sight unseen.

She knew him by the hundreds of letters they had exchanged since the day she turned fourteen years old, some eight years ago. Letters he had faithfully, and hopefully joyfully, written up until one month ago. That last letter—the one telling her he was at last ready to marry, if she was also—was folded deep in the pockets beneath her petticoat, tucked away for safekeeping, like a talisman she could touch for strength and reassurance.

And she needed reassurance now, as the coach rolled to a stop, and the grey gravel crunched under the grooms feet. This was the moment it all began—the life she had been waiting, preparing, planning to lead.

From the backward facing seat, Papa beamed at her. "You look beautiful."

"And you *are* beautiful." Beside her, mama gave her words an entirely different, but no less heartfelt, meaning.

"Thank you. Thank you both." Greer knew she was not a conventional beauty—she was too-flamed haired to be considered pretty anywhere but Scotland—but she knew she was loved. And she knew that gave one a different sort of beauty—a beauty that came from confidence in one's merits.

And if her knees were knocking together, it was from excitement, not apprehension. Because the day had at last come for her to meet the man she loved. Any moment now, Ewan Cameron, His Grace the Duke of Crieff was going to throw open his doors, and greet her with the smile she had been waiting eight years to receive.

She herself was already smiling in readiness, happy to receive him, at last.

And yet, he and his smile did not come. The door remained closed.

"Curious," was all papa said before stepped down from the coach, and took a fraction of a moment to straighten his coat. "Robert," he instructed the footman, "pray ply the bell and inform them that his grace's betrothed has arrived."

She certainly felt as if she had indeed arrived—in more ways than merely standing on the doorstep of her soon-to-be-new home. Greer sat another moment or two, admiring the beautiful proportions of the Palladian mansion, and buff stone balance and pleasuring symmetry. Ewan had described it so perfectly she felt like she were coming home instead of coming to a place she had never been.

On the seat beside her, Mama took her hand and gave her a reassuring squeeze.

"It's quite alright, Mama." She made herself everything calm and unruffled, like a swan gliding along the top of the water, while beneath all was determined work. "I am sure it will all be right as rain."

"Good girl." Mama patted her silk and lace clad arm. "No need to fret or fash."

And yet there was a need for…something.

She had expected that he would have set up a signal from the gatehouse, and been out on the forecourt waiting for her—she would have been, if their situations had been reversed.

"Come, my dear." Papa handed her out just in time, because the huge oaken door finally opened to revel a man in black who must be the house steward.

He was just as Ewan had described him—thin, angular and proud, with a stoic demeanor. "My leddy." He bowed deeply at the waist. "I welcome ye to Crieff."

"Thank you." Greer very composedly smoothed down her embroidered silk skirts, and moved toward the door on her own, as papa handed out mama. "You must be MacIntosh. His grace has told me so much about you."

The man looked so pained that for a moment Greer feared she had said the wrong thing. "His words were everything complimentary," she assured him.

"Thank ye, my leddy." But somehow he looked more anguished at such a compliment.

It was most awkward.

"You are quite welcome. I know I shall come to value you just as greatly as his grace does." And speaking of her duke. "And his grace?"

The steward pleated his lips between his teeth. "It pains me, my leddy—"

"I am here."

Greer turned and felt the warm smile freeze to her face.

This couldn't be her Ewan. Nothing about the sharp-faced, unsmiling man in the grey powdered wig and black embroidered silk suit—which, by the way needed tailoring to make it fit him properly—was familiar. His hair was not blond. His eyes were not green. He was not so tall and ungainly that he might frighten children, as Ewan had once told her he was.

And furthermore, no spark of welcome, no soft flare of recognition lighted his eye. Everything was stiffness and unease.

"Welcome to Crieff, my lady."

He was as correctly polite and formal as if they were strangers. As if she did not already know the private longings of his heart, and he hers.

Greer curtseyed because she knew she should, and because several other men, Creiff's—and very soon her own—retainers had come out into the forecourt. But she could not keep from asking, "Are you Ewan Cameron?"

Perhaps it was her patent disbelief, but there was a twinge, a twitch of narrowing at the corner of his clear blue eyes, as well as a clenching along his jawline, before he covered his discomfort with a pleasant smile. "I am his grace."

Which was not what she had asked.

Because she had been raised to be everything polished and polite, Greer did not allow her annoyance to show. But neither did she falter—she stuck to her point like a burr. "But you are not Ewan Cameron. You cannot be." Everything about him was wrong—different. Unless…

An unwelcome, entirely disloyal thought jumped into her head—what if all his letters, all the words she had cherished and practically memorized for the past eight years, were a lie?

His answer was another almost imperceptible twinge— this one at the corner of his wide, mouth—before the man finally spoke. "No," he admitted. "I am Murdock Cameron, his cousin, and Duke of Crieff now." He looked away, as if he did not like to meet her eyes. "Ewan Cameron is dead."

THANK YOU FOR READING

Thank you for reading *Mad For Love!*. I hope you'll take a few minutes out of your day to review this book – your honest opinion is much appreciated. Reviews help introduce readers to new authors they wouldn't otherwise meet.

THE HIGHLAND BRIDES

Mad For Love is an introduction to The Highland Brides. While each book reads as a stand-alone, the series is best enjoyed in chronological order.

Mad for Love
Mad About the Marquess
Mad, Bad, and Dangerous to Marry
Mad Dogs and Englishwomen

To keep up to date on The Highland Brides, sign up for Elizabeth's newsletter and get exclusive excerpts, contests, and more
http://www.elizabethessex.com/contest/

BOOKS BY ELIZABETH ESSEX

Dartmouth Brides
The Pursuit of Pleasure
A Sense of Sin
The Danger of Desire

Reckless Brides
Almost a Scandal
A Breath of Scandal
Scandal in the Night
The Scandal Before Christmas
After the Scandal
A Scandal to Remember

ABOUT THE AUTHOR

Elizabeth Essex is the award-winning author of the critically acclaimed Reckless Brides historical romance series. When not rereading Jane Austen, mucking about in her garden or simply messing about with boats, Elizabeth can be always be found with her laptop, making up stories about heroes and heroines who live far more exciting lives than she. It wasn't always so. Long before she ever set pen to paper, Elizabeth graduated from Hollins College with a BA in Classics and Art History, and then earned her MA in Nautical Archaeology from Texas A&M University. While she loved the life of an underwater archaeologist, she has found her true calling writing lush, lyrical historical romance full of passion, daring and adventure.

Elizabeth lives in Texas with her husband, the indispensable Mr. Essex, and her active and exuberant family in an old house filled to the brim with books.

Elizabeth loves to hear from readers, so please feel free to contact her at the following places:
E-mail: elizabeth@elizabethessex.com
Web: http://elizabethessex.com
Twitter: https://twitter.com/EssexRomance
Facebook Page:
https://www.facebook.com/elizabeth.essex.37
Pinterest: https://www.pinterest.com/elizabethessex/
Goodreads:
http://www.goodreads.com/author/show/4070864.Elizabeth_Essex

Made in the USA
Charleston, SC
06 April 2016